THIS ONE'S GONNA HURT

CODY J. THOMPSON

Black Rose Writing | Texas

ISBN: 978-1-68513-155-5
PUBLISHED BY BLACK ROSE WRITING
www.blackrosewriting.com

Printed in the United States of America
Suggested Retail Price (SRP) $20.95

This One's Gonna Hurt is printed in Garamond

*As a planet-friendly publisher, Black Rose Writing does its best to eliminate unnecessary waste to reduce paper usage and energy costs, while never compromising the reading experience. As a result, the final word count vs. page count may not meet common expectations.

For (evil) Matt and Tabitha.
Thank You for showing me that horror can be beautiful poetry.
I hope I make you proud.

Makre sure to check out
Cody J. Thompson's first novel

THRILLER

LIBRARY
COPY

Bone
Saw
Serenade
A Novel
Cody J. Thompson

"Channeling his inner Raymond Carver, Thompson sets in motion a
complex flashback narrative structure that involves past jealousies,
betrayal, and the worst in humankind."
–Rex Pickett, Academy Award Winner
and author of *Sideways* and *The Archivist*

THIS ONE'S GONNA HURT

CHAPTER 1

The sky transformed as the sun began to set over the western hillside in the barren California desert. Like all of us, our magnificent sun must put itself to rest each evening, enabling it to provide life for plants and animals alike the following day. Each morning, it awakes and emerges from the east, providing warmth, life and energy to our beautiful, blue planet. As warm beams of light cut through the wispy clouds scattered across the sky, they create an exquisite and picturesque mosaic. Changing from their typical bright white and gray to a gorgeous mix of sky blues, purples and pinks resembling giant patches of delicious cotton candy. Far away, yet appearing so close, one could almost reach out and pluck a strand right from the sky and enjoy its sweet, decadent flavors.

Danny Padilla, a Latino man in his late 30s, gazed up at the colorful sky, his eyes locked in on the carnival of colors as they rained down upon him and his family. His jet-black hair combed back in slick fashion while boasting an unshaven face from many busy days that were now behind him. Speeding down the 15 freeway was the entire Padilla family in their trusty Toyota 4 Runner. Its silver paint showcasing a sort of chameleon effect from the kaleidoscope above. Behind the SUV was a U-Haul trailer packed to the brim with the Padilla family's possessions. The Padillas were headed West from their longtime home in Henderson, Nevada to Orange County. For years, it had been the family dream to move closer to the beach and milder temperatures of Southern California, and that dream had become reality.

In the passenger seat sat Danny's wife, Jennifer. Her long, dark brown hair pulled back underneath a cheap-looking New York Yankees ball cap. A perfect ponytail had been pulled through the snapback of the hat, which now flopped back and forth along with the motion and movement of the car. With her tired face buried deep inside a good book, she hoped to burn through a couple of chapters before the sun retired for the night. In the back seat, the Padilla children sat quietly, joining in their father's wonderment at the colorful sky above them. 8-year-old Bobby looked away first, returning his attention to a tablet sat upon his lap as he played a video game. One of those games where kids could build different worlds, only to attack - or be attacked - by another player's army that set his parents back a good 3 dollars. 5-year-old Gracie, strapped into a protective booster seat, continued to watch as the clouds drifted their way across the sky over the mountains in the distance. She giggled to herself as she attempted to pick noticeable farm animals out of the colorful cloud shapes.

The family hadn't been on the road long, only recently breaking over the Nevada border into California. Still, they had many hours of drive-time before reaching their destination - their brand-new home in Orange County. The family couldn't be happier about their big life move. Waves, consistent weather year-round and, as lifelong Disney fanatics, Danny and Jennifer had already pre-purchased annual passes for the entire family to Disneyland. They hadn't shared the news with the kids, yet, as they hoped to surprise them with a visit to the Happiest Place on Earth once they settled in and unpacked. There's always enough excitement and uncertainty that comes along with moving to a new city and state. They didn't want to get the kids in a tizzy along with the packing, unpacking and a long drive through the night in between.

"You're really jamming through that book, huh?" Danny asked his wife with a smile.

"Yep," she replied bluntly. "I would make even *more* progress if you would stop interrupting me."

She looked at her husband with a sly smile and a friendly wink. Their relationship surprised many, as cracks like this were commonplace.

Though never mean spirited, it was all in good fun. It was how they communicated. How they showed love, as odd as that may seem to the untrained eye or ear.

"Well excuse *me*, Ma'am," Danny said back with the perfect level of sarcasm.

"It's getting really good and I have little daylight left," she said, adjusting her position in the seat. "We left so late. I'll just be sitting here bored once it gets dark."

"Well, you can always sleep on the drive. It's been a long couple of days. And the work is only just beginning."

"Don't remind me," she said with a roll of the eyes.

"Oh, stop it. It's going to be perfect. It's worth it."

"I know, I'm just so tired," she said, as her body gave out a long yawn.

"Exactly. See? Might as well get some rest. Nothing else we can do except count the lines on the freeway. And that's no fun, right?" He asked the kids in the back.

A collective "Yeah" came from two unenthusiastic, tired children in the back of the SUV.

"Aren't you the least bit excited to move to California? Everyone wants to live in California."

"Of course, I am," Jennifer said. "Don't mistake my exhaustion for anything less than excitement."

"Good," He said with a smile. "It's going to be great."

"Hey, Dad," Bobby shouted, not looking up from the intoxicating light coming from his tablet screen.

"What is it, champ?"

"I need to pee."

Danny looked into the rear-view mirror at his son, and then back to the road. There was nothing but landscape around them as they drove. Cactus and sand stretched for miles on either side of the freeway, without a shopping center, mall, or even a rest stop as far as the eye could see.

"Are you sure? You can't hold it, son?"

"No, Dad. I need to go *now*," He said, adjusting his position in the seat as an exasperated look washed over his childish face.

"Shit," He said under his breath, his eyes scanning the surrounding desert.

"Hey, language," Jennifer said in an intense whisper.

"Well, I don't know what we're gonna do. I don't see any gas stations or anything, do you?"

Just then, they passed a green sign positioned on two large 2x4s on the side of the freeway. They were approaching an exit where Danny hoped maybe they could stumble upon a convenience store - or something - for a quick bathroom trip. And if he were being honest, he could use a caffeine boost, anyway.

"There we go," He said, pointing out the windshield. "Halloran Summit Road. There's an exit about a mile up."

"I don't see anything in the distance that would provide a clean bathroom for our children, do you?"

"Maybe we'll get lucky," He said, clicking on the right blinker. "Stand by, buddy. Put a clothespin on it, OK? We'll find a place as soon as we can."

The SUV slowed at a stop sign that sat at the end of the off-ramp for Halloran Summit Road. A random off-ramp on the 15 freeway, which seemed incredibly odd for Danny and Jennifer. It appeared there was nothing out there. No tall, glowing signs shooting into the sky, like most exits on long road trips, advertising overpriced diesel and proclaiming to serve "The World's Best Coffee." From where they sat, it seemed like a long-forgotten piece of land in the middle of the desert that one could assume hadn't been touched by another living soul in decades. Danny turned left off the ramp and headed down the road, deep into the isolated area.

After driving for a good while, to Danny's surprise, he came across a small, well-lit parking lot. The parking lot looked brand new, with its black asphalt almost shimmering underneath the light poles which were positioned around its perimeter. The lot was as random as it could be, as it didn't provide parking for any business in sight. A park and ride, maybe? But all the way out here? Who would trek this far off the beaten path? The only structures nearby were an old, crumbling building that resembled a once busy mechanic's garage and snack shop, and in the distance stood three run down trailers. Plumes of white smoke rose from behind the trailers, though there was no life to be seen outside of the Padilla family. Danny pulled the SUV and trailer into the lot and set the car in park before shutting down the engine.

"Why are we stopping? Where are you going to go?" Jennifer asked.

"This place is as good as any," He assured her. "He can pee behind that building. What does it matter? There isn't anyone around. No cops. It'll be fine, right buddy?"

"Sounds good to me," Bobby said with excitement as he unbuckled his seatbelt and pushed the back door open.

"Honey," Jennifer said with caution in her voice. "I don't know if I like this. It seems creepy. And what's with that smoke billowing up behind that trailer? This is way too sketchy. Let's find somewhere else."

"Where else are we gonna go? There isn't anyone around. Who cares about that smoke out there? Those trailers are probably burning down and that isn't our problem. Besides, if someone lives out here, we'll stay as far away from them as possible," he said, stepping out of the car. "Desert people are fucking weirdos."

CHAPTER 2

Danny, with his right hand gently pressed into Bobby's back, ushered him across the smooth pavement as they stepped onto the desert sand and rushed towards the abandoned building. The right side of the building was equipped with a couple of roll up doors that one might assume housed everything needed for a mechanic shop - Car lifts, chests filled with tools, large shelving units displaying oil cans. To the left, an old convenient store or snack mart for road weary travelers to load up on salty snacks and ice cold sodas. The entire structure appeared as though a bomb had been dropped on it as it disintegrated and rotted in the unforgiving desert sun. Though it was still standing, there wasn't much to say - or salvage - of the building. The outside walls were covered with graffiti and other forms of vandalism from past occupiers or desert weirdos looking to blow off steam. Surrounding the building was a low, cinder block wall that stood just low enough for an adult to step over. The surrounding ground was nothing more than sand, dirt, and weeds that had accumulated from years of abandonment.

When they reached the wall, Danny lifted Bobby from under his arms up and over. When his little sneakers hit the sand, Danny stepped over to join him.

"Let's head around the back to do our business," Danny said, pointing to the end of the building. "Make it quick. Your mom is nervous and wants to hit the road."

Jennifer remained in the car with Gracie, keeping an eagle eye on those trailers in the distance and the unexplained smoke from behind them that continued to climb high into the air. Looking to her right towards the building, she noticed that her husband and son had snuck around the back and were now out of her sight. As she peered back at the trailers and the smoke, she bit the fingernails on her right hand. She'd always had this nervous habit - One she'd tried to break. But it always seemed to creep back without her even realizing she was doing it.

"Come on, come on," she whispered to herself.

"What's wrong, Mommy?" Gracie asked, holding a small doll in her hands. She bounced it up and down on her legs as though it was performing a dance number without a care in the world.

"Oh nothing, kiddo," she assured her daughter. "Everything's fine. As soon as your father and brother get back, we'll be on our way to our new home. Are you excited?"

"Yeah!" Gracie shouted.

"Good," she said, continuing to bite her nails. "Me too."

The boys stood side by side, with a rusty old gas pump between them. Danny finished his business first, as he only tried to go as a precautionary measure. He buttoned his jeans, pulled his belt tight and took a few steps away, as he stared out at the vast desert before him.

"Hurry it up, Bobby," He said, running his left hand over his slicked back hair. "We need to get back to your mom. I don't want her to chew her fingers to the bone."

He placed his hands on his hips and allowed the cooling desert air to wash over him. It felt great, and he began relaxing his body as he gazed out at absolutely nothing at all. The entire landscape was eerily calm and serene. It took little focus to hear the wind blowing through the area, whipping through the tall weeds, creating a cascading sound that took over his senses. As Bobby wrapped up his business, the surrounding air changed in an instant as an unfamiliar sound whooshed through the air.

THWAP!

A dull thud soon followed the sound. Like the thud in a deli when a butcher slaps a side of beef on the counter. Then, something that resembled the sound of air escaping through liquid filled the silence. Bobby turned to look towards his dad, when the sound changed again. This time, it shifted to terrified screams.

Lying on the sand was Danny, fighting for oxygen as blood gurgled out of his mouth and down his right cheek. He gasped for air, unable to breathe as he began to drown in the blood that had flooded his throat, and now flowed into his lungs. Sticking through his neck was a small arrow. On the right side of his neck, a metal arrow tip showed about an inch through his now ripped skin. The arrow had torn straight through his flesh and throat, decimating everything in its path. He rolled to his back as he fought with all the power he had to fill his lungs with oxygen. He blinked his eyes feverishly as he pressed his hands deep into the sand. His fingers curled in and out, making little fists in the sand as though he tried to grab onto something - anything - for leverage. As his life poured into the sand, his face turned white. The rapidly escaping blood pooled around his shoulders in the dirt, creating massive black clumps that resembled fresh tar.

Bobby's entire body shook with fear. For a moment, his little brain didn't know what his body should do. He was teetering on the edge of falling into shock. Finally, a small burst of courage hit his little feet, as he turned to run towards his mother. Though his efforts were useless. As he twisted his body to the right, his face connected with something so hard that it sent him stumbling back a couple of steps. When he focused his terrified eyes, he saw a stranger standing between him and the abandoned parking lot. His eyes were wide open, his jaw unhinged and falling towards the ground. The shock had taken hold of his body and mind as he became paralyzed with tremendous fear where he stood.

Just then, the stranger lifted his right hand into the air, holding a rusty old meat hook. The stranger swung it downward with immense force, connecting the pointy end with the top of Bobby's head. The sound of shattered bone echoed over the landscape as Bobby's little brown eyes rolled to the back of his cracked head and his body went limp. As the stranger pulled his arm upwards to tear the hook from Bobby's head, his small body followed as his little sneakers lifted from the dirt. The stranger held Bobby in the air at eye level and as his body slowly pulled away from the hook. As his body fell to the ground below, a long string of sticky blood and brain matter followed, like a wet, crimson spider web stretching from his head to the curve in the hook. Once his head cleared the hook, his lifeless body crashed to the ground, landing next to his father.

Jennifer continued chewing away at her nails, her eyes locked on the 3 trailers in the distance. She again looked over her right shoulder towards the back of the building, yet there was still no sign of her husband or son.

"Come on," she muttered. "What is taking them so long, huh?" she said with a nervous laugh, hoping to not worry her young daughter.

They sat together, Gracie unaware of her mother's growing anxiety, in absolute silence. To Jennifer, those few moments felt like years. Until the silence was broken, startling her to her very core. A loud *CLICK* bursted through the silence as the locks on the SUV engaged on their own.

"What the hell?" She asked out loud, reaching to unlock the passenger door.

Just as her fingertips unlocked the door - *CLICK!* - They locked themselves again. She turned and looked over her right shoulder, letting out a gasp that was from so deep within it shot a bolt through her entire body. Standing at the edge of the old building was a man. A stranger. He was terrifying, dressed in a butcher's smock and pointing Danny's set of keys at the car. The man continued locking the doors in an attempt to keep the girls locked inside. She reached to her feet, grabbing a black leather purse on the floor of the SUV. She began rummaging through, searching for the second set of keys. As she fought through the contents within her handbag, the back passenger side window shattered, raining shards of glass over Gracie's body. Gracie began screaming and crying so loud, one would think a lung might fly out of her mouth and land right on her lap. The glass cut ribbons of her arms and face, as blood trickled out of the fresh gashes that now covered her body and head.

Jennifer screamed as tears poured down her cheeks. She found the other set of keys inside her purse. She repositioned herself upon her knees on the passenger seat, turning around to comfort her crying, bleeding child.

"Baby, baby!" she screamed, reaching for Gracie. "Oh my god! Oh my god! We've gotta get out of here!"

She froze, as her eyes locked on the stranger. Now, he was sauntering towards the car with a crossbow held in front of his face. It was pointed at Jennifer, an arrow locked and loaded, ready to rip.

"Fuck, fuck," she whispered to herself.

She jumped across the center console, wrestling her body into the driver's seat. Shaking, she tried to get the key into the ignition. All the while, Gracie continued to scream and howl in excruciating pain, being too young to understand what was, or could be, happening to her and her family.

Jennifer fumbled with the keys when another loud *THWAP* echoed through the air. An arrow passed through the broken window, over Gracie in her booster seat, and stuck into the side of the driver's side chair, just missing Jennifer's head.

"Come on! Come on!" Jennifer yelled, not looking back at the stranger.

Finally, she got the key into the ignition and cranked it with every bit of strength she could find. The engine kicked over, and she threw the SUV into drive, smashing her right foot into the gas pedal. As the car jolted forward, she turned the wheel to the left, hoping to get out of the parking lot and head towards the freeway to safety, or really, to anything but this. Before she could turn the car away, another arrow flew through the air, entered through the broken window, hit the steering wheel, and fell onto Jennifer's lap. The arrow had a soft tip on the end and was engulfed in flames. She began swatting the arrow when she noticed the smell of an accelerant. Whatever liquid had doused the soft tip was now all over her hands and arms, resulting in flames that began covering her skin and burning her clothing. She screamed while trying to drive and put the flames out at the same time.

She took her foot off the gas as she tried to extinguish the flames that grew over her entire body, when the car's momentum slowed to more of a crawl. Another flaming arrow entered through the broken window, this time connecting with the back of the driver's seat. Flames grew upwards toward the roof as they engulfed the inside of the vehicle.

"It's OK Gracie! It's OK honey!" She screamed through the pain as she continued to flail her arms about to extinguish the flames. The accelerant had coated her skin so much, the flames continued to grow over her body and her clothes caught, covering her entire body with bright orange flames. She couldn't hide the pain or fear any longer and began screaming for help, but it was useless.

One last *THWAP* sound shot through the air, as one last arrow entered through the back window, striking Jennifer in the right side of her neck. It stopped halfway through her throat, and blood poured out of her mouth, down her chin towards her burning shirt. Her black and singed hands reached painfully for the arrow, as her body convulsed so hard she could no longer control it. She planted her feet into the floorboard, pressing the gas pedal to the floor. The SUV shot forward as it gained speed, until it collided head on with an old, wooden pole that sat on the side of the road. The SUV came to a halt as the back tires continued to spin and burn, sending plumes of burning rubber into the air. There, the car sat, wheels spinning but unable to move, as flames overtook it. Soon, the flames hit the gas tank, blowing the car to pieces, as well as the Padilla girls.

A large fireball shot high into the night sky, followed by thick, black smoke. There were no more screams or cries for help. The only sound left to fill the silence was the crackling sound of intense fire as the car was reduced to nothing more than a blackened shell to rot in the sand.

CHAPTER 3

"Jenna, Spencer," Brad yelled over his shoulder towards the house, clicking a key fob pointed at the driveway. "Let's get going already. I want to hit the road some time this *century*, alright?"

Brad, a senior at Bay Bridge Academy, strutted across the front lawn with a backpack strapped over both shoulders. He was a burly teen, well known throughout the Bay Area as a star athlete in many track and field events. A handsome guy with chiseled biceps, pecs and a sharp jawline to match. His brown hair had been styled to his precise specifications; just spikey enough to let unknowing folks understand there might be just a dash of douchebag sprinkled over his personality. He was decked out in a pair of black Bay Bridge PE shorts, a "Property of Bay Bridge Academy" t-shirt and white socks pulled up high that disappeared into a worn-out pair of black Vans shoes.

In the driveway sat a brand new, polished and pristine vehicle. It's black paint shimmering and sparkling in the morning sunlight like a glittery gymnast's uniform - A Zeus Model X-1.

Zeus Auto Makers was the producer of the latest and greatest electric vehicle that money could buy. If your pockets were deep enough, that is. Luckily for Brad and his sister, Jenna, their father, Thomas Miller, could afford this modern marvel of luxury automobile. The Zeus X-1 was sexy and sleek, with a flowing, low profile body that sat close to the ground. It came standard with large, sporty rims wrapped in low-profile tires, making the car look that much hipper. The car ran on electrical power only, so it would go without saying that it required charging to run. But, for most commuters, each full charge could take a driver close to 500 miles when driving the X-1.

A deep, clunk sound filled the air as the trunk hatch popped open. Brad reached down, lifting the hatch door high into the air, removing his backpack as he went, tossing it inside.

"Geez, Brad," Jenna shouted with a deep sigh as she marched across the front lawn, a blue duffel bag draped over her left shoulder. "Calm down. Quit rushing us."

Jenna, much like her older brother, was a star athlete on the Bay Bridge track team. She was only a year younger than her brother, though if someone claimed they were fraternal twins, anyone would believe it. She was tall and Brad looked like the male version of her, almost as though the Miller's had used a cookie-cutter for their two teenage children. Strong genes in the Miller pool, some might say. She wore black yoga pants and a loose tank top, showcasing her athletic, toned body. Her auburn hair pulled back into a lackadaisical ponytail.

"If I don't keep pushing you, we won't leave until this evening. I know how you work."

"How I work? What's *that* supposed to mean?" Jenna asked, her face squinched as she tossed her bag into the trunk next to his.

"Come on," Brad said, his left hand still resting on the open trunk hatch. "You'll need two more bathroom trips. Somehow, an extra makeup application will be involved. I know. It'll be an entire *thing* with you."

"Up yours," Jenna barked, smacking his stomach with the back of her hand. "You sexist jerk."

"Hey, I call em like I see em," He joked. "Where's Spencer?"

"I don't know. Inside, I guess," Jenna said, ending any eye contact with her brother.

"You mean you're not keeping an eye on his *every* move?"

Jenna glared up at her brother, annoyed yet concerned what he may say next, and that Spencer could emerge from the house at any moment and hear the entire conversation.

The Miller's house was a gorgeous, old-world colonial style home. Tall, crystal clear windows wrapped the exterior and opened the home to the majestic morning sunshine and crisp breeze of the San Francisco bay. A quaint porch of red brick steps led to the front door, which was framed perfectly by 4 colonial columns that held an upper-level deck overlooking the front of the property. Vibrant white, with navy blue trim, the house was the gem of the neighborhood, showing off just how successful the Miller family was. The house, along with the pricey Zeus X-1, made the Miller's the envy of the neighborhood - or the scorn - depending on who you asked and on which day.

"I don't know why you won't just be honest with the guy," Brad asked. "*Everyone* knows you've got a crush on him. Just tell him."

"I can't just *tell* him," she said, batting her eyes in nervous fashion.

"Why? What's the big deal?"

"I'm not stupid, maybe?"

"How is it stupid to tell someone you have a crush on them?"

"Quit pressuring me," Jenna said through clenched teeth. "I'm not like you, OK?"

"Trust me, I know. If you were, you'd already be in those pants."

"See what I mean? I'm not stupid," she said, her eyes now staring dead into his. "Like *you*."

"Hey, what you see as stupidity, I see as confidence."

"I *am* confident that you *are* stupid."

Just then, Spencer came bouncing out of the house and down the front steps, slamming the front door as he exited. Spencer was the same age as Brad, and had been his best friend since they were little kids. He wasn't an athlete, or even considered "cool" like Brad was. Regardless, their friendship worked. In the end, that's all that mattered to either of them. Not popularity or athletics, but how they meshed as friends. Spencer was what some folks might consider "nerdy". With his curly hair that somehow grew upwards, he was rail thin, tall and had a charming, yet obnoxious goofy streak in him. He approached wearing loose fitting jeans, a plain, faded blue t-shirt and a rubber Bill Clinton Halloween mask resting on top of his head. A backpack flung over his left shoulder.

"Shut up," Jenna muttered, pushing a strand of hair behind her right ear. "Just be quiet."

"Don't be such a spaz," Brad said.

"Stop it, he's going to hear you."

"I'm going to hear what?" Spencer asked, dropping his backpack into the trunk.

"Oh," Brad said, staring at the sky as though an explanation that wouldn't embarrass his sister might fall from the clouds and land in his mouth. "Just that, uh, Jenna hates your mask. She thinks that it's dumb."

"Brad!" Jenna shouted, punching him in the right shoulder.

"Ouch, bitch!" He shot back.

"You don't like my mask?" Spencer asked, shocked. "I think it's funny."

"No, it is," she said. "Brad's just being a dick, like usual."

"What did I say?" Brad asked.

"Whatever, *I* think it's funny," Spencer said. "Anyway, I still can't believe your dad is letting you drive his brand new Zeus to Vegas for the weekend."

"What he doesn't know won't hurt him, will it?" Brad asked with a wink.

"Wait, you're hijacking your dad's *brand new*, 120,000 dollar car for a road trip to Las Vegas?" Spencer asked, leaning backwards with a full belly laugh.

"See, I told you this is a stupid plan," Jenna remarked, her arms crossed in disapproval.

"First of all, you shut up," Brad said, glaring at his sister. "Secondly, he'll never know. He's in Europe with mom for the next 2 weeks. We'll be back safe and sound before they even come into the country. Besides, he's fucking clueless."

"He's going to notice the miles, Brad," Jenna said.

"Bullshit," He replied with a cocky giggle. "He's so up his own ass, he won't even realize anything has been put on."

"You don't think he's going to notice over a *thousand* extra miles on his brand new car? He loves this thing more than he loves us."

"No chance," Brad assured.

"Well, if he does, this entire plan was *your* idea. Remember that. I'm not taking the fall when he freaks the fuck out on you," Jenna said, serving as a verbal agreement.

"Whatever, I don't give a shit. I'll be off to college in a few months anyway, and he can't torture me anymore. What's he gonna do?"

Just then, a brand new, beautiful white BMW came rumbling up the long driveway, coming to a stop just to the right of the X-1. The windows were down, allowing the unrestricted sounds of the latest popular electronic music to fill the air of the neighborhood.

"Damn, finally," Brad shouted with an agitated sigh. "I was starting to think you didn't want to come with us."

The driver was Lexi, Brad's long-time girlfriend. Her long, voluminous blonde hair that radiated in the morning sun flowed like a gorgeous stream on a postcard down her head to her shoulders, with perfect streaks of natural brown hiding away underneath. She wore high, athletic shorts and a Bay Bridge Academy hoodie that was zipped only halfway.

Much like the Miller's, Lexi's family resembled something you might see in the background or a deleted scene from *Vanderpump Rules*. Fresh, new money in the Bay Area, and much like the Millers, they loved to flaunt their status all over town. Lexi took pride in her family's success, almost as though the success was her own. Like it was something she herself had earned. She had an attitude for days, with an odd sweet streak that hid just underneath all the fakeness and vanity which she portrayed.

Stepping out from the passenger side was Valerie, Jenna's best friend. Valeria, like Jenna, was on the track team. She was Latino, with beautiful black hair tied up into a messy bun that sat on the top of her head. She wore purple leggings that stopped at her ankles, black Converse All-Stars and a black pullover sweatshirt. Walking in line with Lexi towards the Zeus, each of them carrying their own luggage.

"Hey babe," Brad said, wrapping his right arm around Lexi's waist, pulling her in for a kiss. "Is that *my* sweatshirt? Didn't I ask for this back?"

"You can have it back after the weekend," she said with a cute smile, kissing him again. "I need it to keep me warm during those cold Las Vegas evenings."

"Actually, Las Vegas isn't that cold in May," Spencer shouted matter-of-factly as he opened the passenger side door. "In fact, it's rather warm, believe it or not."

"Nobody *asked*, Spencer," Lexi barked, smacking gum in her mouth and refusing to look in his direction. "Hey, why does Spencer get shotgun? I thought *I* was getting shotgun?"

"He called it!" Brad shouted, his hands in the air. "Those are the rules, babe. What do you want me to do about it?"

"Tell him to vacate the seat ASAP. That's what you can do about it, *Brad*."

"No can do, babe," Brad said, slamming the trunk shut. "Rules are rules. If we abandon them now, all we have left is chaos. Besides, you'll love some girl time in the backseat."

"Whatever, Brad," she snapped, pulling away from him. "And don't call me babe."

"Lexi, wait," Brad said under his breath, motioning for Lexi to step away from the group. "Did you remember your inhaler? I don't want you to suffer—"

"Can you not?" Lexi said with clenched teeth, shooting fury from her eyes to his. "How many times do I have to ask you not to bring that up around anyone?"

"What's the big deal? It's an inhaler. Do you know how many people need one? You shouldn't be embarrassed."

"Well I *am* embarrassed, *Brad*! I don't want anyone to know, OK?"

"I don't see the problem."

"Look, I don't expect you to understand. But this is something nerds and dorks have. Someone like, I don't know, Spencer. Spencer should have asthma. Not someone like me."

"But you do, Lexi," Brad said, running his hand down her arm with sweet intention. "Don't be ashamed. It's not something you can control."

"Still," she said, crossing her arms in disapproval. "Keep it down, alright?"

"Fine, fine. Just tell me you brought your inhaler, OK?"

"Of course I brought it. I always have it."

"OK, good. See? Was that so hard?"

Lexi had been diagnosed with asthma when she was a very little girl. It was something that always embarrassed her. Something she refused to admit to anyone. Brad only found out when she suffered an attack one afternoon during a beach trip. She had been tackled by an enormous wave, which sent her spiraling into the sand. With Lexi, everything needed to be perfect. And somehow, she felt being seen with a condition, even asthma, was enough to shatter the illusion of perfection which she had strived so hard to achieve.

Lexi huffed with a roll of her eyes as she smacked her gum and walked around the car.

"Hey Valerie," Jenna said with a smile, hugging her. "I'm so glad your Mom let you come with us."

"I know, right?" Valerie said with a glowing smile. "It came down to the second, too. By the way, thanks for picking me up, Lexi."

"Hey, don't mention it," Lexi said with a wink.

Unlike the rest of the families, Valeria hadn't been born with a silver spoon in her mouth, or blessed with built in privilege. Amongst the 5, she was the quiet, reserved one. She wasn't showy and had less to show than the others. Valerie was genuinely sweet and caring. The oldest of 3 kids, her sole parent - her mother - worked for a new, exciting tech start-up to take care of the family. Her father had passed away in a horrible accident at one of the many San Francisco piers the year before, where he worked as a longshoreman. A freak accident that left the Gutierrez family devastated, and Valerie's mother with a new and deep-rooted passion for safety and security. Both for herself and, more importantly, her three children. It did not thrill her, the thought of her daughter taking a weekend road trip to Las Vegas, as she called it, "unsupervised". But, as Valerie told her - many times over the past few weeks - she was a big girl and promised over and over not to get into any trouble. The ultimate promise that seemed to make the most difference in the end - a promise not to drink or smoke anything on the trip. Valerie knew deep down this promise was a promise meant to be broken, and she was certain her mother knew it. But a parent planting the seed of disappointment sometimes is enough to grow a flower of obedience and keep a child out of trouble.

Jenna opened the passenger side back door, holding it open for Lexi to climb in. Once in, she slid all the way over to the driver's side, claiming the window seat for her own.

"Hey, Jenna," Valerie asked through whispers, waving her away from the car. "Does Lexi, how do I ask this? Does she know about Brad and me? You know, from the party last year?"

"Oh boy," Jenna said with a nervous giggle. "Absolutely not. No chance in hell she knows about any of that."

"Oh, thank *god*," Valerie said in relief.

"No. If she ever found out, she'd kill you and Brad. And then she'd kill me for knowing and not telling her."

"And Spencer?"

"Well, she'd kill Spencer just for being Spencer," Jenna said as she nervously rubbed the back of her neck. "I don't think many people would need a reason for that."

"It's just, I don't know her that well. She's part of that, how do I say it—"

"The cool kids' crowd?" Jenna said with a smile.

"Well, yeah. You and I aren't *cool*."

"Neither is Spencer, and he's coming. Come on, it'll be fine. You'll have *fun*. I promise."

Valerie nodded before climbing into the backseat and finding her place right in the middle of the backseat which would be her new place for the next 8 plus hours. Jenna climbed in after, slamming the door shut as she went.

The five of them were about to embark on the hours-long journey from San Francisco to the highly anticipated festival Electric Daisy Carnival happening in Las Vegas. Electric Daisy Carnival is a 3-day music festival focusing on electronic dance music. The festival, known for its electric performances, no pun intended, was also known for its fabulous light shows, fireworks displays and the wildest costumes guests could dream up. The festival kicked off on Friday. Since this trip would begin on a Thursday morning, the group could realistically arrive with enough time to get themselves settled - and find some trouble - well before the festivities got underway.

"Alright, everyone in?" Brad yelled, opening the driver's side door and taking his seat. "Strap in, kids. We've got a long trip ahead of us. So I hope you're comfortable. And if you're not, that's your fucking problem."

The car flipped on, though anyone around would have no clue, as the car was absolutely silent upon startup. Without hesitation, Brad shot in reverse down the long driveway. Once the wheels hit the asphalt, Brad turned to the right and sped down the road. It was Vegas or bust, and this group was ready to cash in on a weekend filled with partying, dancing and anything else they might find along the way.

CHAPTER 4

With Brad at the helm of the Zeus X-1, the group flew down the freeway at record - albeit semi-dangerous - speeds. They crossed the Bay Bridge into Oakland as they made their way out of San Francisco. They sped down the I-580 which would soon turn into the I-5 South and become the path until they reached the town of Bakersfield, which was still hours away. Like the beginning of most road trips, rousing conversation filled the air as they drove. The beginning of road trips always seem to be filled with unbridled happiness. The anticipation of the unknown on the horizon. Leading to nothing more than still air and dead silence at the tail end, when travelers have to leave the fun behind them.

Excitement, happiness and anticipation of the unknown infected each of their minds and radiated throughout the air. They knew they were in for the experience of a lifetime in Las Vegas, and each of them was more eager than the next to fill their eyes and minds with the glitz and glam of the bustling city in the desert.

"You know what would be a billion dollar idea?" Spencer shouted with great enthusiasm as he shoved his hand deep into a Pringles can. "If Pringles got into the gift wrap business."

Brad turned to stare at his friend with confusion, as the three girls sitting in the back filled the air with "*What the fuck*" from their eyes.

"What the hell are you talking about, Spencer?" Lexi asked, her eyes squished in disapproval.

"Think about it," He replied, his mouth full of sour cream and onion chips. "They already have the tubes, right?"

"What's your point?" Brad asked.

"If they made their tubes *longer*, they could wrap the outside with gift wrap, and fill the inside with chips. You could wrap gifts *and* have a built-in snack."

"That's maybe the *stupidest* idea I've *ever* heard," Lexi barked.

"A stupid idea?" Spencer asked, shooting around, looking into the back seat. "You're telling me you've never needed a quick snack while wrapping presents?"

"Uh, no," Lexi said with a frustrated laugh. "I think I can make it through wrapping gifts without needing a snack."

"What about you two?" Spencer asked, motioning towards Jenna and Valerie.

"I don't think it's such a bad idea," Jenna said with a lack of confidence in her voice.

"What a surprise," Lexi replied with a roll of her eyes.

"What's that supposed to mean?" Jenna asked.

"Oh nothing."

"Jenna knows what's up," Spencer said as he turned to face the road ahead. "What about you Val?"

Valerie remained silent for a moment as she looked around the car, searching her mind for the right answer that may not insinuate a full-blown argument in these early stages of the trip. The group would be stuck in this confined space for many hours, before sleeping and hanging around one another for 3 straight days. Only to climb back into the car for the long trip home. Valerie hoped they would all get along and remain friends during and after all of this.

"Sure, I guess that's a good idea," she said with caution in her voice. "I don't think I, personally, would pay for that, though. If we're being honest."

"See? It's stupid," Lexi said.

"Oh, come on! A Pringles can the size of a roll of wrapping paper? Are you kidding me? 120 square feet of gift wrap and inside, 6,000 delicious chips await? Sounds like a dream come true to me," Spencer said, chewing rudely on the salty snacks.

"I think you're going to have to buy them separately, bro," Brad chimed in. "I don't see anyone buying something like that. It's ridiculous."

"Well that's a loss for everyone involved, if you ask me," Spencer said, defeated.

"Yeah, look," Lexi said, leaning forward and pushing her head and shoulders between the two front seats. "As interesting and *fantastic* as it is to dream of a 3-foot tube filled with potato chips. Do you two brilliant minds think we can put on some music? We've got a long way to go. And with a conversation like this, I might just *hitchhike* to Las Vegas."

She pushed herself away using the back of Brad's seat as her propulsion device. It was apparent to Brad that she was trying to make a point and get his attention with the same thrust.

"OK, OK," Brad said, rolling his eyes as he leaned his body to the right, reaching into his left pocket to retrieve his cell phone.

The inside of the Zeus X-1 looked like a spaceship, with the area on other cars that would otherwise contain air conditioning knobs, various buttons for radio, an oversized touchscreen had completely replaced other controls. The screen itself was gigantic, taking up most of the space that would otherwise be the center console. Everything to control the vehicle had its own techy looking buttons on the touchscreen to control air conditioning, heat, and entertainment. Because of the luxury of the X-1, it even had high-tech buttons for heated and cooled seats, phone controls and "*so much more*," as the highly animated commercial which advertised the X-1 proclaimed.

Brad reached for the screen and began the process of pairing his cell phone with the computerized car. Once paired, everything he would do with the phone could be controlled and handled through the spacey touchscreen, making hands-free much more possible - and safer - for a comforting, easy ride.

"Yes, Ma'am," Brad said through sighs. "I'll put on some music."

"Don't call me Ma'am," Lexi shouted, punching the back of his seat. "It makes me feel like an old woman. I *hate* that."

"Quit giving him fuel," Jenna said. "You know he's only going to do it more if you keep telling him it bothers you."

"Oh shut it," Brad said as he clicked away at the touch screen. "I'm not that big of a dick."

"Yes, you are," Jenna said. "You're a bigger dick than I'm even giving you credit for."

The rest of the group laughed at Brad's expense.

"Up yours, Jenna. Maybe you can hitchhike with Lexi. What do you think about that?"

"Hey, fuck you," Lexi shouted, again punching the back of his seat.

"OK, you're *seriously* gonna need to stop hitting my seat," Brad said, looking into the rearview mirror.

"Then start being nice to me," Lexi said, with just the cutest amount of coyness in her voice.

"Yeah, dick," Spencer said. "Start being nice to people, why don't you?"

Just then, Spencer shot forward slightly in his own seat. He shot around to look behind him to see Val with a half-crooked smile on her face.

"Did you just kick my seat?"

"Yes," Val shot out, sitting forward. "You need to start being nice, too."

"What the fuck did I do?" He asked, turning back to face the front.

Again, his body popped forward, as a sense of annoyance washed over his otherwise goofy face.

"Last one," Val said through laughs. "For good measure."

Jenna turned to her right, burying her face into Val's shoulder as she tried to hide her laughter. She may have had a crush on Spencer, but in her eyes, Val was her sister. And she would side with her any day of the week. Besides, who doesn't love some good, old-fashioned playful fun?

"I'll remember that," Spencer said, shaking his head.

"Enough fooling around," Lexi said as she leaned forward yet again. "Babe, give me your phone. I want to play the new DJ Max 90 record."

"Nuh-uh," Brad said, waving his finger in the air. "I don't think so. No one gets to just pick whatever they specifically want to hear. That isn't fair. We're going to play a new game on this road trip."

"I've been so excited for this!" Spencer shot out, pounding his closed fists onto his thighs.

"OK, smart ass. What's the game?" Lexi asked.

"We're going to play a new road trip game I like to call - Swift."

"Swift? What the fuck is that?" Asked Jenna.

"This sounds stupid," Val chimed in.

"Well hold the hell on. Let me explain the rules before you pass judgment," Brad barked towards the back seat. He continued, "You know those big rigs we see on the freeway?"

"Yes, Brad. We've all seen big rigs before," Jenna said with just the right amount of attitude.

"You didn't let me finish, smart ass. These are *specific* big rigs and the trailers have a giant logo painted on the side that says '*Swift.*' It's a trucking company. I think Taylor Swift's dad owns it."

"No, that's a myth," Val corrected him. "That rumor was squashed a long time ago."

"Be that as it may, it still fits for the purpose of this game. OK, so hear me out. At the beginning of the game, we start with Taylor Swift music, beginning with her first album."

"You mean the country shit?" Lexi asked.

"Yes, starting with track one on her first record. We continue playing the entire Taylor Swift discography in order of each album until someone spots a Swift truck on the road."

"Then what happens?" Val asked.

"The first person to spot a Swift truck has to yell out the word '*swift*'. When someone does this, they get to turn Taylor Swift off and choose *whatever* music they want, and we all have to listen as we drive. *No complaining*, either. Fair is fair."

"Oh, that actually *is* fun," Val said with a smile, looking to Jenna for approval.

Brad then reached for the dash control screen, pressing play as the song "*Tim McGraw*" - the first track off of Swift's first album. In an instant, the song began blasting through the speakers.

"Well, what happens if someone sees the truck, chooses music, but then someone *else* spots a Swift truck?"

"Then *that* person can turn off the music that had previously been chosen for their own music choice. But," Brad said, holding his finger in the air. "If the chosen album ends before another Swift truck is spotted, then we go right back to where we left off in the Taylor Swift discography. Therefore, everyone has the same chance of choosing their own, favorite music. And if no one spots a Swift truck, the music is pre-chosen. So there will be no arguing or fighting over what we listen to."

"That sounds fair," Jenna said, looking back to Val, as they both shared a nod.

"Yeah, I like this game," Val agreed. "Besides, I love Taylor Swift. So, it's OK with me if we have to listen to her the entire drive."

"Well," Lexi said, sitting forward. "You won't like this game for long. Swift!"

On the other side of the freeway, a speeding big rig shot by. The trailer showcased a huge SWIFT logo that wrapped the entire trailer.

"DJ Max 90, please," she said, settling back into her seat with a devilish smile across her face. Lexi 1 - Everyone else, 0.

CHAPTER 5

The traffic was sparse as they cruised down the I-5, to the CA-58 and finally to the I-15, which led the way straight into the glistening lights of Sin City. Throughout the trip thus far, the car was filled by scattered chatter, some slight bickering and of course, a very raucous game of *Swift*. Lexi had won the first round, followed by a long stretch of freeway without a single sighting of the now holy grail of big rigs. When they first transferred onto the I-15, Spencer claimed to have spotted one as it rushed by on the opposite side of the freeway. Though Lexi was certain he was full of it and trying to get away with something. Which, if they knew Spencer, he probably was. Even though the record was already more than half finished, Spencer's insisted on replaying Taylor Swift's record "*1989*" in its entirety. Nothing pleased Spencer more than a good-natured joke, and he found it hilarious to not only win a round of Swift, but to force the other passengers to hear more Taylor Swift. He didn't care to, or even want to listen to that record. What he wanted to hear were the overpowering groans of his closest friends. A true goofball by nature, yet with a heart of gold.

As the sun fell behind the horizon, they approached the tiny desert city of Baker. The town of Baker was a small, dusty desert town whose major claim to fame was the World's Tallest Thermometer and the home of the Mad Greek Restaurant. It was one two-lane highway in and out, with a population of under 800 people. Aside from the thermometer which stretched high into the desert sky, the town was known as a quick stop to or from Las Vegas. A simple place along the highway to fill up on gas, sodas, and relieve ones-self from the last bladder buster they had picked up at the stop prior to Baker. It wasn't much of a destination. But the small town did its job well and had for many years. The music lowered as a computerized, futuristic woman's voice rang out from the car speakers.

"IN ¾ OF A MILE, EXIT ONTO BAKER BLVD. THEN TURN LEFT."

"Why are we exiting?" Jenna asked, stretching her arms and letting out a yawn so deep, it must have come all the way from her toes.

"We need to charge up a bit," Brad replied, clicking on the turn signal.

"The car needs a charge already?" Lexi asked, mild annoyance bubbling up with her attitude.

"We've been driving over 8 hours," Brad explained. "The Zeus needs a bit of a boost."

Brad drifted the car to the right and exited onto Baker Blvd. The road turned inland for a moment, before jetting to the left, up and over the bustling freeway. This single road was the primary thoroughfare for Baker. Truckers, families and other travelers all stopped into Baker to gas up, hit a restroom, grab a milkshake and to stare at the tall thermometer in the middle of town. Once the road straightened, they could see all the old, sun-burnt buildings and towering signs ahead of them making up the mysterious little town. On the left, just up the road, was a large truck stop with a gas station and small shop attached. The car slowed before turning left into the parking lot. At the far end, butted up to the vast desert beside it, sat two electrical vehicle charging stations. Brad pulled up to the one on the left and turned the car off.

"Alright, perfect," Brad said, smacking the steering wheel with both hands. "So here's the plan, gang. It takes about 45 minutes to an hour to get a decent charge on the car. That should get us to Vegas with ease.

Once we get there, we can leave it plugged in the entire weekend. So, I figure, we plug her in, grab some dinner and then head out. Sound good?"

"Aye Aye, captain," Jenna said as Val laughed along.

"You want to be left in Baker? Huh, smart ass? Maybe the Mad Greek is hiring bathroom attendants."

"Oh, shut up," Jenna said. "I'm just busting your balls."

"How about I bust your head?" Brad said with a playful laugh, opening the door and exiting the vehicle.

As much as these two played into the idea of a spirited sibling rivalry, they loved one another deeply. It was all a part of their relationship. Good-natured trash talk keeps a family together and strong. That was their motto, anyway.

"What have we got to eat around here?" Spencer asked as he stood in the parking lot, stretching his lower back. His face aimed straight to the sky above.

"Nothing pretty," Jenna said as she looked up and down the road.

"Jesus," Val chimed in. "Denny's, Arby's and Dairy Queen? It's like the town that God forgot around here."

"And the Devil's presence can be felt, that's for sure," Jenna joked back.

"We *are* close to Death Valley, after all," Spencer added.

As the others searched for a suitable place to eat a quick dinner and stretched their cramped muscles from the drive, Brad began plugging the Zeus into the charging station. Once the plug was installed in the car's side, he stepped back with his hands in the air, as though he cautiously awaited a shock to himself. He stared as nothing happened. Both the charging station and the prestigious X-1 remained silent, showing no signs of connectivity whatsoever. No acknowledgement on the touchscreen, no beeps were heard - Absolutely no sign of life.

"What the hell, man?" Brad asked, looking over the charging bay. "It's like this thing isn't turned on or something."

"Do you need to pay for it? Is there a debit card slot on that thing?" Jenna asked.

"No," Brad said, running his hands up and down the thick, hard, plastic body of the unit. "These are supposedly free to use."

"Should we check inside and ask the clerk?" Spencer shouted from the other side of the car. "Maybe it's like the tire machines. If you ask nice enough, they usually turn them on for you."

"Yeah," Brad said with a hint of confusion in his voice. "Anyone want to come in with me?"

"We think you can handle this mission on your own, Captain," Jenna joked.

"What did I tell you about being a smartass?"

"Not to be one?"

"And?" Brad asked as he began walking towards the mini-mart at the other end of the parking lot.

"I decided to do it anyway," Jenna said with a laugh.

Brad walked through the parking lot feeling defeated. He pulled open the metal and glass doors that led to the mini-mart, as a bell crashed and clanked around against the glass as it swung. The inside of the store, with its bright, obnoxious, yellow tile, fluorescent lighting and wall to wall snacks resembled every convenient store most people have seen or visited on a long drive. It wasn't anything special, but for the road weary traveler, it was more than enough. The smell of lemon disinfectant and overused bathrooms filled the air of the interior. Every roadside mini-mart always appears the same. Decaying fixtures, colors so frightening that it hurts to look at them and there always seems to be an all too familiar rank odor. Almost as though it's some sort of insane federal law for a store to smell this way to remain open to the public. Maybe it was a lack of care. Maybe it was to prevent loitering. Either seemed more than possible. And regardless of the reason, it was true, and never pleasant.

"Excuse me," Brad said loudly to the clerk.

"What's up, man?" The clerk asked.

He was a young townie wearing an oversized red polo shirt with the gas station logo embroidered on the left chest. His arms were covered with tattoos in an odd placement that looked like they were done in a prison cell. His mop of greasy hair fell over his face and he had large gauge holes in both of his ears.

"Do uh, the charging stations outside work? I plugged in, but it doesn't seem to do anything."

"Which one did you plug in to?"

"The one on the left. I think it had a '1' sticker on it."

"Oh yeah," The clerk said, staring down at the counter. "That one, like, doesn't work."

"Oh, OK. So, does the other one work? Charging station 2?"

"Nah man," The clerk said, swatting some undistinguishable dust and crumbs off the counter to the floor below. "They're both turned off."

"Uh, OK then," Brad said, halfway turning around. He then turned back, "Is there any chance you *can* turn them on? We're on our way to Vegas and we won't make it without some juice."

"Sorry, bro. I think someone is coming to check them out next week."

"Well, shit. Is there another charging spot in town?"

"Nah," The clerk said, in a long drawn out fashion. "Sorry again, bro."

Brad shot the glass door open with a burst of anger, as the bell clinked and clanked again. He walked with a level of intense agitation back to the car to break the news to the group.

"Well, we might be in a bit of trouble," Brad said, running his hand over the top of his head.

"What's wrong?" Lexi asked.

"The charging stations aren't working, and they won't have anyone to look at them for a week or so."

"Shit," Spencer shouted. "So, what are we gonna do?"

"You have your phone?" Brad asked. "Search around us and see if we can find any charging station behind us, or maybe at a rest stop down the freeway that we can use. We still have *some* juice left, but not much. If there's a station close, we should be able to make it."

"Dumbass," Jenna shouted. "I told you to bring your own car. We could've just gassed up and been on our way by now. But *no*, you *had* to take Dad's new Zeus."

"Do *you* have money for gas? Huh? Multiple fill-ups along the way? Plus, hotel and everything else that comes with a weekend in Las Vegas? I was trying to save us *all* money."

"Well you'd better figure this one out," Jenna said, her arms crossed in anger. "I'm not getting stuck in this hell hole of a town."

"Hey, everyone shut up, I got it," Spencer yelled, holding his phone up into the air. "A few miles down the road, off Halloran Summit Road. This California Travel website says they have charging stations."

"Is there anything else off that exit? *Good* food, maybe? I'd prefer to not have food poisoning as we roll into Vegas," Lexi remarked, her attitude on full display.

"Nah," Spencer confirmed. "It looks like it's in some sort of small park and ride or something."

"A park and ride in the middle of nowhere? Why would they put that there?" Val asked.

"Who cares? It works out perfect for us," Brad shouted with enthusiasm.

"How is that perfect?" Lexi asked, her arms crossed as the desert air grew chillier by the second.

"No buildings probably mean no people," Brad said, his face taken over by a devilish smile. He looked to Spencer and continued, "No people, that means—"

"Oh, hell yeah!" Spencer shouted, reaching out for a high five from his friend.

"What are you two idiots talking about?" Jenna asked.

"It takes, what, 45 minutes to an hour to charge her up? We can grab some snacks from the mini-mart, hang in the desert for an hour. And, show them Spencer," Brad said, nodding his head.

"Biggity blam!" Spencer shouted, removing a sandwich bag from his pants pocket with a handful of rolled joints inside. "Plus, I snagged a bottle of rum from my old man's liquor shelf and we acquired some fireworks."

"Are you two fucking serious?" Lexi asked, stepping back from Brad.

"What's this big deal? We can smoke and drink a bit and shoot off some fireworks. It'll be a fucking blast! And a perfect way to kill time and get the weekend started, if you ask me."

"I don't know, you guys," Val said cautiously.

"Don't worry so much, Val," Spencer said, wrapping his left arm around her shoulder. "We're gonna have some fun, and we will show you the ropes. Let's start this epic weekend off with a literal bang."

"Come on, it'll be great. I bet the hour will fly by like that," Brad said, with a snap of his fingers.

CHAPTER 6

One after another they filed into the mini-mart to stock up on supplies for what they hoped would be the last leg of the drive. Each of them was hit by the offensive mix of lemon cleaner and heavily trafficked lavatory as they entered. The aromas swirled about in the air thanks to an overhead blower positioned just above the double glass doors. Anytime the doors were pushed open, the blower kicked in, shooting whomever was unlucky enough to stand below in the face with the offensive odors.

"I'm going to use the restroom before we roll out. Anyone with me?" Brad asked.

"Good call," Spencer agreed. "You girls may want to go as well. I don't think they've got clean facilities in the desert, partners," He said in a mock John Wayne accent.

"We're good, but thank you," Lexi said mockingly.

The three girls meandered through the store, stocking up on snacks and cold drinks for the drive as well as the hour wait that was now ahead of them. Val picked out an acai Vitamin Water and a bag of Flamin Hot Cheetos. Jenna, a random, unknown energy drink, some peanut M&M's and a bag of Nacho Cheese Doritos. Lexi, an expensive, pretentious bottle of water, a couple packs of spearmint gum and a Tootsie Pop. Jenna and Lexi were the first to approach the counter with their snacks and drinks. Lexi had unwrapped the Tootsie Pop and began eating it in the store, swirling it around within her cheeks and over her tongue, pulling it out of her mouth resulting in many loud smacks and pops. They set their items onto the counter as the tattooed clerk began ringing them up.

"So," Lexi asked, swirling the tootsie pop in her mouth. She pulled it out aggressively again, resulting in a loud *POP* sound. "Are you going to hook up with Spencer on this trip?"

"Oh my *god*, Lexi," Jenna said as she blushed.

"What's the big deal? We *all* know you like him. And he clearly likes you. I mean, shit, he would be stupid not to. You're hot."

"Really? You think so?"

"Hey, I'm not trying to hook up with you. But if I swung that way, count me in, sugar," Lexi said, bumping her hip into Jenna. "No, but seriously. Are you going to defile the little dork or what?"

"Well," Jenna said, brushing her hair behind her right ear. "I don't know. I *probably* will. I don't see why not."

"That's my girl!" Lexi shouted, patting her on the back. Her eyes landed on a small wire display that sat on top of the counter next to the register. "What's this? Herkey Jerky?"

Sitting on the counter was a white wire frame stand showcasing different flavors of beef jerky from a brand called Herkey Jerky. Small, plastic bags were positioned on the display, each one filled with multiple strips of seasoned beef.

"Have you ever had that stuff?" The clerk asked, as animated as he had been maybe in his entire life.

"No, I've never seen it before. Is it any good?"

"Oh shit," The clerk said as he placed his hands on his head in disbelief. "It's the best jerky you'll ever eat. Trust me."

"Oh yeah?" Lexi said as she held up a bag, admiring it.

Inside the clear plastic bag, one could see many slices of tender jerky. On the front, colorful sticker labels had been placed with the words Herkey Jerky in a fun and playful font. Next to the lettering, a funny looking character of a man with a mustache held a thumbs up with a mile-wide grin.

"This looks cool. And hey, look, it's made here in Death Valley. Is this stuff made locally?"

"Oh yeah, not too far from here," The clerk admitted. "The guy who makes it brings in cases once a week himself and we buy it directly from him. I'm addicted to the stuff. I eat a bag every day, man."

"Hmm. Should I get some?" She asked, looking at Jenna. "Fuck it, I'm going to get some. Couldn't hurt to fill up on some extra protein, right?" She pulled the lollipop from her mouth again, producing another rude POP that filled the air. Lexi grabbed a clear bag with a green label that proclaimed it was the sweet and savory flavor.

Brad and Spencer finally arrived at the counter, their arms filled with different goodies for their enjoyment; Multiple cans of Pringles, Reese's cups, sunflower seeds.

"And a 2-liter of Coca-Cola," Brad said, slamming it onto the counter top. "For the rum, of course."

"Hey, did you bring a lighter with you?" Spencer asked.

"Shit, I don't think so."

"It's all good. I'll buy one. I could use a new Zippo, anyway."

Next to the Herkey Jerky stand sat a display of souvenir Zippo lighters. Spencer spun it around a couple of times before he found one that fit his liking. A gold Zippo with a giant American flag on the front.

"Eh? What do you think?" He asked.

"Why that one?" Lexi asked.

"To go with my Bill Clinton mask. Come on, it's funny."

Everyone shot out a collective roll of the eyes at this joke that had crashed and burned at his feet. He continued to go about his day with that dopey mask pulled up on top of his head, wearing it like a ball cap. No one had thought to ask why. Mainly, because it was Spencer. And his explanations were almost never worth the trouble of asking.

"What's the damage, my friend?"

"That'll be $38 dollars."

"Anyone have any cash?" Brad asked as he looked at each of them.

"Cash? Who carries cash?" Lexi asked, twirling the tootsie pop in her mouth.

"A lot of people carry cash. You don't carry cash?"

"No, I don't carry cash, *Brad*."

"Forget it, it's on me," Spencer said as he swiped his card. "You can all thank me later."

"Yeah, you remind us to do that, will ya?" Lexi said, picking up her items and heading towards the door.

"Thank you, Spencer," Jenna said. "That was really nice of you."

They shared a smile as their eyes met before leaving the sickening stench of the mini-mart behind and exiting into the chilly, evening air.

As they each piled back into the car, Lexi tore open her bag of fresh jerky. Without hesitation, she reached inside, retrieving a rather large slab of dried, flavored meat. It was a dark brown color with shades of auburn and white marbling throughout. It was damp to the touch, letting the consumer know just how fresh it truly was. As the bag remained open, the car took on aromas of sweet honey and savory teriyaki. Lexi tore at the slab of dried meat, pulling a generous morsel with her teeth as she chewed loudly.

"Oh, wow," Lexi said, her eyes wide open as she chewed. "This is *fantastic*. That weirdo clerk wasn't kidding."

"It smells fucking epic," Brad said, his nose up into the air like a hungry dog. "Let me try a piece."

"Anyone else want to try?" Lexi asked as she handed a slab to Brad in the front seat. "It's *really* fucking good."

"Sure, I'll try a small piece," Jenna agreed.

"Val? Spencer?" Lexi asked, tearing off a small piece for Jenna.

"No thanks," Val said, waving her hand at Lexi.

"I'm good," Spencer said.

"Whoa," Brad said as he chewed away at the moist morsel of meat. "You were *not* kidding. That's the best jerky I've ever tasted. There's so much deep and complex flavor. And the texture is *insane*."

"Seriously," Jenna gushed. "Shit, on the way home, we should stock up on this stuff. I've never tasted anything like it."

"I wonder if they ever send any up our way?" Lexi asked, tearing another morsel with her teeth.

"Doubt it," Jenna said as she chewed. "He said the guy brought it in himself to sell."

"Then I agree, we'd better bring some home with us. It'll be great after my Pilates class on Wednesdays," Lexi said, her mouth full as she spoke.

The car chugged down the freeway and began showing signs of shutting down just as they finally hit Halloran Summit Road. Brad flicked on the turn signal, swerved to the right and cruised up the ramp, exiting the freeway. At the top of the minor incline, he hung a right and followed the glowing strips in the middle of the road deep into the dark and desolate desert. Finally, they came across a small, empty parking lot. A steel pole stood at the end of the asphalt that said —

HALLORAN SUMMIT PARK AND RIDE.

The pavement of the lot looked brand new. It showed no signs of cracks from the desert sun or pressure from other vehicles that had stopped prior. It was illuminated by what appeared to be newly installed street lamps, one on each corner of the small lot. Next to the empty lot stood what was once a convenience store, gas station and mechanic's garage, though it had long been abandoned. Shooting up high into the sky was a rusting pole, with an old, decaying sign on top with burnt out neon letters that read HALLORAN SUMMIT MARKET AND DIESEL. The sign served as a gravestone to the long-forgotten business.

The building resembled an old gas station with a mechanic shop on one side and a convenience store on the other. In its heyday, one could imagine this may have been a bustling truck stop for long road truckers and road trippers to and from Las Vegas or beyond. Now, the building was crumbling more and more by the minute, its outer walls caving into itself. What was left of the exterior was covered in graffiti and different types of vandalism from past visitors. It clearly had closed many years ago, and the sun and elements have long had their way with the empty ghost of a building. Nature has a way of taking things back for itself, and nature had claimed this building long ago. The lot itself comprised only 12 parking spots, 4 of which were equipped with charging stations. The car puttered along and stopped in front of the one furthest to the left.

"Damn, I think we just barely made it," Brad said, letting out a deep sigh of relief and running his right hand over his head. "Alright, folks. We've got ourselves about an hour. How about we make the best of it? What do you say?"

"Might as well," Jenna said, not excited about the situation ahead of them. "Can you plug my phone in to charge, please?"

"That reminds me," Brad said, reaching for the glove box. "I got this adapter so all of our phones can charge. Might as well let them fill with juice while the car is plugged in, right?"

Each of them plugged their cell phone into the charging block before they exited the car. They began stretching yet again underneath the bright fluorescent lights. Each of them surveyed the area in their own way, as Brad fussed with the charging station. This one, unlike the last stop, wasn't free. A charging session at this park and ride would set them back an even $20 for an hour of charging. Brad swiped a debit card and entered his pin when the LCD screen gave the approval for charging to begin. He pulled on the cord giving him enough length to shove the charging handle into the port on the side of the X-1. The screen on the tower lit up with a small image of a sedan, as a black bar moved from the trunk to the hood. The bar moved back to front repeatedly, showing that the charge had in fact begun.

"Hey look at that, we're in business," He said.

"Great," Lexi said sarcastically. "So, you say we should be here, what? An hour?"

"Give or take," He assured.

"Good. Because this place isn't creepy, like, *at* all."

"I agree," Val said, her arms crossed as she looked out towards the deep darkness that lasted for miles all around them. "It's really dark out. I'm kind of freaked out here."

"Ah, don't be," Brad said, dismissing their concerns. He clicked open the trunk and began rummaging through the bags. "It'll be fine. Besides, Spencer and I took precautions. We've got plenty of things to pass the time. We'll be out of here and back on the road before we know it."

CHAPTER 7

Brad pulled a duffel bag from the trunk, throwing it over his right shoulder before slamming the hatch with his left hand. He walked with purpose through the group as though he was parting the sea with his mind and movement. The group watched him go, then followed along like he was some sort of devilish cult leader. Once Brad's feet left the smooth asphalt and hit the desert sand, he dropped to one knee, setting the bag on the sandy floor. In the same motion, he unzipped the bag and began rummaging through the contents within. A bag of tricks for unsupervised, teenaged amusement.

"Let's see what we have here," he said as he began pulling items from the bag. "We've got red cups and Spencer's rum that he stole from his dad. Thank you, Spencer."

"Not a problem, Captain," Spencer said, tipping the Bill Clinton mask which still sat on top of his head like it was a baseball cap.

"We've got a 2-liter of coke to go with the rum, of course. We have some beautiful, and I mean *beautiful*, premium weed to smoke. And, the cherry on top of it all," Brad said, smiling over his right shoulder at the group. "Fireworks anyone?"

Brad lifted a long, cellophane bag and held it high into the air, like he was hoisting a championship trophy over his head. Inside the bag was a bundle of roman candles. On a recent adventure day trip between Brad and Spencer, they had come across an illegal fireworks stand on their way to Santa Rosa. They had acquired enough fireworks and explosives to light that entire parking lot with colorful sparks and fire for hours. Before the drive, they decided to bring only the roman candles on this trip, thinking that would provide plenty of amusement. Besides, they didn't want to blow their entire stash in one day. And seeing as they were now driving across state lines in a car that had been borrowed without permission, they knew, if pulled over and searched, the weed and rum was enough to thrust them into deep water. The boys had no desire to add any unnecessary troubles to their wrap sheet if a nosey cop found their car stocked with a trunk full of illegal fireworks. Solid teenager logic, of course. Now, they no longer cared about the repercussions as they planned to mix all three at once out in the open on this dark and lonely evening.

"Oh god," Jenna said, rolling her eyes and turning her back to her brother.

"What's the problem?" He asked.

"Dangerous much?" She added with a very apparent attitude. "You want to get high *and drunk* to shoot off fireworks? What if we start a fire?"

"Look around us. How are we going to set anything on fire? It's wide open for miles and miles. What's going to burn? The sand?" Brad replied as he tore at the cellophane wrapping around the fireworks.

"Sounds fucking *fun* to me," Lexi said, reaching for the bottle of rum that sat idle in the sand.

"That's the spirit," Spencer added as he began handing out red plastic cups.

"I don't know," Val added. "I'm with Jenna. This all seems a little crazy. Besides, don't you have to drive in an hour?"

"Don't worry about me. I'll keep it light. More for all of you, anyway," Brad said as he stood up and handed two roman candles to each of them.

"Hold out your cups," Spencer ordered.

Spencer filled each cup with a generous portion of rum. Lexi followed behind topping each cup with chilled coke.

They stood in a circle formation in the sand, each with a red plastic cup filled to the brim with rum and coke.

"Spencer, gimme that Zippo you bought," Brad said.

Spencer reached into his front pants pocket before tossing the American flag lighter to his friend.

"Alright, folks. What do you say we get this fucking party weekend started!" Brad yelled. As he finished his sentence, they reached into the circle, slamming each other's cups together before they each took a few generous gulps. Unbeknownst to the group, Brad had lit one of the roman candles, so as they drank, he held his left arm high into the air, as bright red and gold fireballs shot high into the night sky. One after another, the decorated tube fired off the glowing balls of fire. They each began their own brand of hooting and hollering as the sky above them engulfed in shimmering red and gold sparks. They continued to guzzle down the mixed drink until the roman candle fizzled out.

"Alright everyone, you each get two of these mother fuckers. So make them count," Brad said.

"Light me up, Spence!" Lexi shouted.

Spencer flicked the Zippo and ignited the end of Lexi's first, sending bright white sparks into the chilly, desert air.

"Woooo, baby!" Lexi shouted as she began running in circles.

"Me next!" Jenna pleaded.

"Oh, well. Look who wants to join in the fun after all," Brad mocked.

"Shut up and light me, dipshit," she barked back.

Spencer held the lighter as Jenna pushed the tube into the flickering flame. As the tube kissed the flame, the same glowing, white sparks erupted into the darkness surrounding them. Val followed along, as Spencer lit her candle. Soon, Val, Lexi and Jenna all twirled in the sand, their arms stretched well over their heads as glowing balls of fire shot high into the sky before fizzling out. Each shot left trails of smoke behind that remained visible even in the desert breeze.

"Hey, watch this," Brad told Spencer in a whisper.

He lit the end of his second candle and pointed it at the three girls as they danced in a sort of rhythmic fashion together. Flames of green and blue shot out the end like a muscle car's exhaust, followed by many soft thuds as he shot fireballs at their dancing feet in the sand. The girls screamed in a playful nature as they tried to dance out of the way of the red-hot projectiles.

"You can't hit us, you hack!" Lexi shouted through laughter. The others joined in, laughing heartily together.

"Hey, look out there," Spencer said, pointing off into the distance.

Positioned about 100 yards away from the parking lot sat three abandoned trailers. They were propped on stilts above the sand and sat next to one another. They could barely make out details on the trailers, as they were swallowed almost entirely by the darkness of night. It appeared as though they could have been decent trailers at an earlier time in history. Now, they were rusted and beaten beyond repair by the sun, as the wind and sand that pelted it daily without protection annihilated them beyond repair or recognition. Windows on the right side of the closest trailer had what appeared to be curtains hanging on the inside, and steps led to what was once the original front door. Remnants of a once cherished modular home, now left and forgotten to rot in the elements.

"How much you bet I can hit that trailer from here?" Spencer asked.

"With a roman candle?" Brad replied. "Bullshit. They're too far away. These candles wouldn't reach that far."

"Oh yeah? Make a wager on it, tough guy."

"OK. You hit it from here, and I buy *all* of your meals in Vegas."

"No shit?"

"No shit. But you've gotta do it from *here*. No cheating. If you miss it, you're buying my meals."

"You're on," Spencer agreed as he lit one of the remaining tubes.

He held it in front of him as the end engulfed in intense greens and blues, shooting white fiery sparks in all directions. It began firing, and the screaming balls of fire died well before the trailer, fizzling out in the sand. One after another, they failed to reach the intended goal.

"I told you, dude," Brad mocked.

"Fine, I'll get a little closer."

"That wasn't the deal. You take one step closer and you lose, bitch."

"Eh, what the hell do I care? Now I'm on a mission just to hit the damn thing."

Spencer marched toward the trailer, holding the tube far in front of his body. Each shot fell short, like the ones before it, until the tube went cold.

"What are you trying to do?" Jenna asked.

"I want to nail that trailer with a blast," Spencer confirmed.

"Oh hell yeah," Lexi shouted. "Light me up, I want to hit it, too."

Lexi, Jenna, Val and Spencer held their last remaining candle outward, so the ends touched. From underneath, Spencer held the lighter, so each one ignited at the same time. Sparks and different brilliant colors erupted from the ends, illuminating their bodies from underneath, sending shadows across each of their faces as though they were sitting at a campfire preparing to tell each other ghost stories.

"OK. Everyone ready?" Spencer yelled.

The air filled with dull thwacks as the four candles blasted fireballs at the trailer. They stood, shoulder to shoulder, their candles held far in front of their bodies, as the side of the trailer was pelted with missile after glowing missile.

"Take that, you piece of shit!" Val yelled.

"Val!" Jenna shouted with a deep laugh. "What's got into you?"

"Hey, I'm finally in the spirit!" She shouted. "Let's have some fun!"

The four of them continued to shower the trailer with fire, continuing their own personal shouting, laughing and celebrating. What they didn't know, and could not see, was the curtain at the far end of the trailer had been moved aside ever so slightly. A pair of dirty fingers from the inside pulled the curtain away from the glass, as two dark eyes peered out at them, watching their every move. Little did they know, they were not alone. And, though they were not in fact telling horror stories to one another, whether they liked to or not, they were about to experience one of their very own.

CHAPTER 8

After exhausting any fun, or trouble making options they could create in the open, fresh air, the group found a way to sneak into the rotting convenience store. At the back of the building, a heavy door had cracked from the hinges and was barricaded from the inside by metal shelving units. Together, Brad and Spencer dislodged the shelves to create an opening into the building. It was a sketchy opening, but a way in none the less. They found a comfortable enough spot in the middle of the old store and took seats on the debris cluttered floor close to one another. Spencer had removed two pre-rolled joints from the sandwich baggy in his pocket, lit each of them, and began passing them around in opposite directions. They sat, huddled together, puffing and passing the joints, as their minds and bodies loosened and floated to another place.

"You know," Spencer started in, speaking with a raspy voice as he held thick marijuana smoke deep within his lungs. "Whoever designed public bathroom stalls. I don't think they had any regard for the people who would be *using* said bathroom stalls." He exhaled a massive cloud of smoke as he finished the sentence.

"What the fuck are you talking about, bro?" Brad asked, falling to his right in laughter.

"I mean, like. The stall doors don't go to the floor. They *always* have those gaps between the doors and the walls where you can see out, *or in*.

And the locks are always janky. Don't even get me started on the little nubbin locks. I have no confidence in those little nubs."

"You're a little nub, you dork," Lexi said, bursting into laughter as a plume of smoke poured from her lips.

"I agree with you, Spencer," Jenna said, smiling as Brad passed one of the lit joints to her. "I hate public bathrooms. They're always so disgusting. Everything is so wet in there. Yuck."

"Thank you, Jenna," He replied.

"Big shock, man," Lexi said, taking another long drag.

"What's your damage, Lexi?" Spencer shot back.

"Can't you two just hook up already and get it over with? My goodness."

"What in the—" Spencer said, his eyes wide open.

"Lexi, fuck you, man," Jenna blurted out.

"We're all thinking it," Lexi added. "I'm the only one brave enough to address it."

"I sure as shit am not thinking about it. That's my sister."

"Oh whatever," Lexi said, shaking her head. "Moving on, *apparently*. Say, Spencer. Speaking of being the world's biggest dork. What's with the Bill Clinton mask? You've had that stupid thing on the top of your head all day."

"It's funny," He said.

"To you, maybe."

"All of you brought costumes and outfits for the festival, right? It's tradition to dress up. So, instead of showing skin and shaking my privates for everyone, I decided to go the funny route."

"You're going to the festival dressed as Bill Clinton?" Lexi asked, shocked and embarrassed.

Spencer pulled the mask down over his face before he spoke. "You got that right, madam," He said in a terrible Bill Clinton impression.

The room filled with laughter as they enjoyed his poor imitation. Above their heads, an entirely new ecosystem had been born. Puffy white clouds lingered about the room made of thick marijuana smoke. From his left, Lexi handed Spencer one of the two lit joints. He lifted the mask, revealing just his mouth. With the joint to his lips, he took in a deep inhale of the thick, dank smoke. He then returned the mask so that it covered his face. Through the mouth and nose holes of the mask, wispy trails of smoke flowed as he exhaled.

"I did not have marijuana relations with that joint," Spencer said, again, in his awful Clinton impression.

The room erupted with laughter, as each of them fell to their sides laughing at Spencer's expense. Val remained quiet, as she usually did, during the smoke session.

"Val, aren't you going to smoke?" Lexi asked.

"Oh no," she said, waving the joint away. "I'm OK. I don't really smoke."

"You might as well, honey," Lexi told her. "Look around you. You're going to get a mean contact high, anyway. Why not enjoy the experience?"

"Come on Val, you'll be fine," Jenna urged. "What's the harm?"

"You *are* amongst friends, Val," Lexi pressured.

Val thought for a moment, then took one of the joints in her hand. She held it between her index finger and thumb for a moment, staring down at the glowing red tip. Slowly, she raised it to her lips, inhaling the hot, skunky smoke into her lungs. She immediately broke into a coughing fit and fell forward towards the floor.

"That a girl!" Lexi cheered, as the others giggled to themselves. "Now you'll feel fantastic."

The room had already spun for Val thanks to the oxygen being contaminated by the second-hand smoke, and now, she felt like she was on a tilt-a-whirl. The floor seemed off, and everything slowed around her. But she wasn't as afraid or as nervous as she had imagined. To her pleasant surprise, she felt light, alive and warm all over. She felt her mouth change to a halfmoon shape as she smiled to herself. About what? She didn't know. And at that moment, it didn't matter. For the time being, she felt like a part of the group. A *cool* kid. And she liked every second.

"Alright," Spencer shouted, slapping his thighs with his open palms. "I need to go take a piss. Anyone want to join me?"

"Absolutely fucking not," Lexi said.

"I meant Brad, but thank you for chiming in."

"I'm all set, Bro," Brad assured him.

Brad, who had been holding his body up on its side with his elbow, had retired to lying on his back. His right arm outstretched over his eyes, as the weed continued to intoxicate his body and mind.

"Suit yourself. I need to take care of business."

"Try not to get," Val said, stuttering her words a bit as she went. "Im-*pee*-ched, out there."

The group sat silent, giving ample time for the joke to land. Once it traveled from their ears to their brains, they couldn't contain themselves as the room burst with maniacal laughter. Not at Val, to her surprise. But *with* her.

"Wow," Spencer said. "Maybe let's hold off on any more weed for Val."

"Absolutely not," Lexi said. "I say, keep the smoke going. If she's got jokes, I want to hear what else she's got for us. Good work, Val. That was the joke of the day, honey."

Val was pleased with herself. She felt good, she felt happy. And better yet, she felt accepted.

"Alright, I'm gonna go piss on a cactus."

"Ew, gross, dude," Jenna blurted out.

"What's the big deal? I like to pee *on* stuff. So, what?"

"And that's the guy you have a crush on?" Lexi asked in disapproval.

Everyone laughed. Not like they had laughed with Val. This time they definitely laughed at Spencer's expense. An occurrence which he was far too familiar with.

"I've never pissed on a cactus," He said as they laughed. "If that's funny, call me George Carlin."

"Timely reference, bud," Lexi added. "Don't get too close. Your prick might get pricked."

As Spencer approached the back exit, he shot Lexi a boisterous middle finger. He climbed up and over the heavy metal shelves, pushing one leg out, then the other and landing hard on the sandy floor outside. He looked around, when he noticed way off in the distance stood a giant bunch of cacti. "*Jackpot*," He thought to himself, and he strutted into the darkness.

The cactus was far away. Much further away from the building than he felt he should travel alone on foot, but he felt safe. Without another soul for miles, no one could see him, and even better, touch him, as he stood in the pitch-black night. He faced the expansive cactus bush, the tallest part which stood 2 feet taller than him. He unbuckled his jeans and began his comforting release onto the base of the plant. The relief was so comforting that he lifted his chin up into the air, allowing the cool night breeze to encapsulate all of his senses. He took in one deep breath and held it for a moment. Then, he heard something. Or he thought he heard something. A sound over his right shoulder. A clinking of some sort, like steel being dragged across the floor. He turned and shot a look over his right shoulder, but saw nothing. Did someone follow him out of the rotting building? It wouldn't surprise him if someone had, in a sad attempt to mess with or scare him. He thought nothing more of it and continued to relieve himself. As he finished and began buckling his pants, the feel of cold and intense pain startled him. It was a sharp pain from a wire that had been thrust over his head, wrapping around his neck.

Reaching for the cold, steel wire, he pulled his fingers away in an instant, as sharp barbs on the razor wire stabbed into his fingertips, slashing deep. Gasping for air, he tried to scream for help, but before any sound made its way up his throat and out his mouth, he felt a blunt hit into the middle of his back. His body shot forward and his face connected with the cacti as sharp spines began stabbing into his face and chest as he fell. Pressing his hands into the thick stalk of the plant, the spines sliced and dug deep into his palms, fingers and his arms. He tried again to scream as the steel around his neck grew tighter, reaching over his head to find a thick rope stretching from the steel noose that sliced and cut into his neck and throat. Someone, or *something*, behind him pulled harder and harder on the rope and as they did, the barbed wire became so tight, Spencer could no longer breathe. The sharp razors of the wire cut so deep into his throat, his windpipe began filling with blood that now spurted and sprayed from his mouth and lips.

He turned his head as far as he could to look behind him to see a massive figure looming over him. As his eyes landed upon the figure, he watched as they pulled with one strong motion that forced Spencer's body away from the cactus to his back, landing hard upon the desert floor. He continued to fight for breath and wrap his bloody, sliced hands around the razor wire that choked and cut the life out of him. With every grasp and every pull, the rusty blades sliced through the skin so deep that it tickled the bones in his hands and fingers.

Spencer then felt the razor wire as it moved over his skin, slicing his flesh from collarbone to jawline as the man began pulling his body across the sand by the end of the rope. He looked up to see what appeared to be a disfigured, heavyset man pulling the rope behind his chubby body as he walked, dragging Spencer's body along with him. The razor wire continued to slice his entire neck and throat to shreds, as blood poured down his throat filling his lungs. Spencer was drowning in his own blood as he fought for what brief life he had left.

The man continued to drag Spencer's lifeless, bleeding body back to one of the abandoned trailers. He stopped at the stairs and reached for the handle on the front door. Once the door opened, he took one labored step, followed by another, pulling Spencer's deadweight upwards. The sharp wire around his neck tore away at the flesh around his jaw, and up over his cheeks leaving thick, deep gouges as it moved. Once the man entered the trailer, he grabbed Spencer from under his arms and hoisted him inside. He let his body fall, resulting in a deep thud as it hit the floor of the trashed and disgusting trailer. The man wiped his brow, bent over and removed the mask from Spencer's face. He admired it for a moment, and then pulled it over his own head, letting out a throaty grunt as he moved.

CHAPTER 9

The rest of the group continued to sip rum and cokes and puff on the joints while, as far as they knew, Spencer searched for a cactus to relieve himself. Spencer had tossed the sandwich baggy of joints to Brad before he retreated, and Brad, regardless of needing to drive again, soon lit up another. He inhaled deep, holding the thick smoke inside his chest. His face transformed from a pained look, to a broad smile, as he nodded softly, allowing the smoke to pour from his mouth. He passed that lit joint to his left before lighting a second, passing it to his right.

"Careful there, babe," Lexi said with a judging giggle. "Remember, you're driving the rest of the way."

"I'll be fine," Brad said, stretching both arms behind his head, returning to his flat position on his back. "You act like this is my first time."

"You're asking for it, dummy," Jenna chimed in. She lifted one of the rolled joints to her lips, her chest puffing outward from the inhale.

"I'm not asking for shit. Chill out."

"We should save some of these for the festival," Lexi added. "Good way to make friends. Besides, I want to be thoroughly fucked up when DJ Max 90 takes the stage."

"Everyone calm down," Brad said through whispers. His eyes closed. "We're going to fucking Vegas. Weed grows on trees out there."

"You mean, it grows like a weed?" Val joked.

"Whatever," Brad said, unamused and unmoved by her correction. "You got my point. Clearly."

The smoke circle continued in perfect rotation, each one of them puff-puffing before passing the hand rolled devil's lettuce. Their heads moving further and further from any sense of clear thought, they remained unaware how much time had passed since Spencer left them to empty his bladder.

"Jenna, what outfit are you wearing to the festival?" Lexi asked, puffing lightly on what was left of a fading joint.

"Nothing too crazy. I've got these black cut-off jean shorts I'm going to wear and a tie-dyed bikini top."

"That doesn't sound too bad."

"I'll be comfortable, at the very least. What did you bring?"

"Oh wait until you see it," Lexi said, a playful smile washing over her face. "I got a full rainbow dragon costume. But *sexy*, you know? Not one of those high school mascot suits. It definitely shows *plenty* of T and A."

"Well, you've got to show T and A," Brad chimed in.

"Yeah? I'd better not see those eyes of yours shooting out of your skull at any *other* girls T and A," Lexi shot back.

"I've only got eyes for you, babe."

"What about you, Val?" Lexi asked.

"Oh," Val stuttered a bit before continuing her response. "I don't think I'll be going the T and A route. Um, I also have a tie dye bikini top and shorts. But I brought a net shirt to wear over it. I don't know. I'm not as comfortable as you both are with this kind of stuff."

"I can dig that," Lexi said. "No worries. We'll show you how to be a nasty little deviant this weekend. Just follow my lead."

"Right on. You've got plenty of practice, don't you babe?" Brad said as he jumped to his feet. He moved across the room and knelt down as he wrapped his arms around Lexi's shoulders, kissing her on the cheek.

"You fucking pig," Lexi shouted, fighting him off of her. "Jenna and I are strong, independent, *smart* women. We know what we want, and we can do whatever we want with our bodies. So up yours."

Lexi reached forward giving Jenna a friendly high five.

"That's one of the many things I dig about you, babe. Your strength *and* your smarts. But," He said, lowering his voice. "I don't mind the T and A, if I'm being honest."

"The modern-day male, everyone," Lexi said with a condescending smile. "Can't even give a fucking compliment without including the female anatomy."

"Don't hate me because I'm honest."

"No, I hate you because you're a *man*. But, that's also why I love you so much. Your honesty. Besides, I'm not into girls. And if I was, I would choose Jenna. No offense, Val. I don't think you could keep up with me."

"None taken, *at all*," Val assured her.

"So, Sis. When are you gonna make your move with Spencer?" Brad asked. "We all know you two like each other. Just grow a pair and make a move already. It's 2022 for fucks sake."

"I know," Jenna said as she blushed. "I just want him to make the first move. He's so sweet and funny. I don't want to corrupt him. You know?"

"He'll be fine, trust me. That kid could use some corruption," Lexi added. "Say, you should have gone as Monica Lewinsky as your festival costume. That would have like, *guaranteed* a hook up."

"No, I'm good," Jenna said. "Besides, that poor woman has taken enough shit over the last few decades. People should leave her alone."

"Amen," Lexi agreed.

"Speaking of, where the hell is Spencer? He's been gone a long time," Brad asked. His head cocked back, chin into the air looking towards the opening at the back of the building.

They had just noticed that Spencer had been missing for quite some time. Far too long for their liking, as he was alone in the desert. They believed they were alone, but the darkness, the cold and the striking silence of the desolate space could make anyone's mind play tricks on them.

"It's cool. I'll go check on him," Jenna said, standing up from her cross-legged position.

As Jenna walked to the back of the building, Val chimed in to stop her.

"I don't know if it's such a good idea for each of us to keep wandering off alone. Maybe we should stick together."

"Why? There isn't anyone for miles. It's just us out here," Jenna said, confidently.

"I could use some fresh air, anyway. I'm coming with you," Val said, pulling herself to her feet with the help of a steel, mesh display stand that at one time may have held many pastries, cakes or cookies.

"I could use some air myself," Brad said. "Babe? You coming along?"

"Sure, why not?" Lexi said, somewhat let down. "Give me a hand up, you big powerful man, you."

Brad stood, then reached down with both hands towards Lexi. She wrapped her hands within his, and with one quick burst of energy, she jumped up into the air, wrapping her arms around his shoulders. She planted a long kiss on Brad's lips as Jenna and Val turned away from the semipublic display of affection. Jenna didn't need, or want, to see her brother engaged in any form of affection. Public or otherwise.

One by one, each of them stepped out of the building and into the fresh, crisp night air. They turned and headed around the back of the building as the vast, wide open desert stretched endlessly to their right. Darkness as far as the mind's eye could imagine. Well into the distance - one might assume miles - the dim moonlight illuminated massive hills that must have stretched endlessly into the wide open unknown. Now, the mountains looked like black blobs stretching up into the sky. Like the darkest thunder clouds anyone had ever seen were rolling towards them, bringing its storm - and wrath - along with them.

Through the darkness, the group couldn't see much of anything. Once they passed the decrepit building, to their left, they could see the Park and Ride, lit by tall street lamps. Sitting lifeless in the streams of light was Brad and Jenna's father's Zeus X-1 in its state of slumber. Charging away, without a care in the world. Brad, leading the way, stopped when he cleared the building. He put a hand across his brow, shielding any remnants of the fluorescent lamps from his eyes, as he peered, his eyes squinted tight, into the nothingness of the California desert.

"Where the hell is he? Do you see him?" Brad asked.

"I don't see anything," Jenna agreed.

"Spencer!" Brad shouted into the air. Then again, even louder. "Spencer!"

"Spencer, where are you?" Jenna shouted.

"This is fucking stupid," Lexi said, her arms wrapped tight into her body. "It's getting cold out here. Come back already!"

"See, I told you we shouldn't separate," Val said, nervousness creeping up inside her body like a fever.

"Spencer!" Brad yelled again. "If you're joking around, I'm gonna kick your ass, dude. So come out and save yourself from the ass beating of the century."

They continued to shout his name to no reply. All they heard in return was the howling wind as it rolled over the pitch-black hills far in the distance.

"Maybe we should fan out and look for him," Jenna suggested.

"Jenna, we need to stay together," Val urged.

"OK, I think you're both right," Brad said. "Let's fan out some and try to find this moron. But try to stay within each other's sights, OK?"

"Agreed," Jenna said with a polite and confident nod.

"Lexi, go check over by the car. See if he's hiding or something. Maybe he's trying to be funny. If he jumps out at you and tries to be a wiseass, kick him in the nuts."

"Check. I can do that," Lexi said, almost as though she hoped she could in fact kick him in that most precious of areas.

"I'll head out past the parking lot, maybe he walked back that way, away from the building. Why, I don't know. Val, why don't you scope out the building and see if he's around here somewhere. You can stay close and if you need to head back inside, no hard feelings."

Val nodded in approval.

"I'm gonna head out by those trailers," Jenna said as she marched with confidence.

"You sure you're OK over there?" Her brother asked. Caution trembling on every syllable. He loved to bust his sister's balls, but deep down, he loved her. "Val's right. Maybe someone should go with you."

"I'll be fine. There's no one here but us."

She continued her march into the darkness of night before turning back and shouting at her brother. "I'll be careful, I promise."

CHAPTER 10

"Alright. Remember, everyone stays within each other's sights. The car will be done and we should be able to hit the road soon. So, let's find this prick, and hit the road to Vegas," Brad shouted as he stomped through the parking lot.

Against Val's better judgment, they separated and began searching their respective areas. Brad crossed the parking lot, jogged across the road and began searching through the shrubs and weeds for his dopey friend in the plot of land across the deserted street. Lexi climbed on her hands and knees under the car, wondering if he was planning a sneak attack on them from low ground. Nothing there. When she stood, she walked out of the parking lot and towards the crumbling old store. Val kept close to the building. As creepy as she found it, she kept her left hand outstretched, her fingertips just tickling the wall as she walked cautiously around.

Jenna, feeling courageous, walked tall and proud towards the three dark, abandoned trailers, shouting Spencer's name as she went. Not that she was fearless. In fact, this march had her shivering as though a fresh snow had just dusted the ground beneath her feet. Having a - now quite public - crush on Spencer, she felt if she found him, maybe he would fall head over heels for her, his savior. *"My Hero,"* he would shout, as he wrapped his arms around her thin waist, planting a sensual and long-awaited kiss on her young lips. The reward, she hoped, was enough reason to march without fear, into the darkness, to save her man in distress.

She continued shouting his name into the air, though no reply was heard from any direction. As she approached the trailers, she lowered her voice. For what reason, she wasn't sure. Maybe the fear was getting to her, maybe it was something else altogether. Something about searching around any structure does that to people, especially in the dark. Even when trotting through a graveyard, people tend to speak in whispers. Like their outspoken words might disrupt the dead and resting.

"Spencer," Jenna whispered.

She pressed her left hand against the filthy, rust infested wall of the trailer as she walked beside it. She tiptoed her way to the far edge and cautiously glanced around the back. It was darker than dark behind those trailers. Even the intrusive moonlight didn't reach the depths of shadows the trailer produced. When she walked behind it, she felt a burning, intense sour sensation overtake her nose and throat. She covered her nose and mouth with her right hand, as she gagged uncontrollably. The stench emanating from the back of that trailer was unlike anything she had ever experienced. Never having smelt rotting flesh, she could only imagine this must be what people must mean when described. The overpowering smell of rot and dead flesh filled the air, twirling freely with a familiar stench that reminded her of a snuffed-out campfire. An almost sweet, yet somehow putrid aura floated around her. Almost as though Death himself called the trailer home. The smell was almost too much to take, but she pressed on. She needed to find Spencer.

She pushed through the reek and rot that filled the air, as she noticed that the sand below had turned to a sort of thick paste. Her shoes sank deep into the muck and the mud, which seemed to release an even more rank stench into the air. A wet, metallic scent rose from the thick, pudding-like sand beneath her feet. Like heat and stink rising from a sewer grate in New York City.

She pushed through and made it to the edge of the first trailer. Jenna could see there was a small space between it and the next rusted storage trailer that sat just to the right. The ground became so thick and mushy, she had to reach out her left hand, grasping onto the edge of the first trailer, pulling her weight forward. As she pulled her body, she could see down into that small clearing. All the while, she continued to whisper Spencer's name, hoping that if he were hiding close by, he would soon come out.

"Spencer," she whispered. "This isn't fucking funny, man. Come on. This is *disgusting*. We need to get out of here. Spencer, can you hear me?"

She gasped in a moment of fear as she stared between the two decaying trailers. The crawl space between the two was pitch black, as the night had claimed the area as its own. The perfect amount of moonlight could cut through, thanks to an opening at the top of the two containers. In that dim moon beam, Jenna saw what appeared to be an eyeball staring out at her. She jumped back when the face staring back at her adjusted, revealing the stupid mask Spencer had been wearing all day.

"Spencer, you fucking asshole," she shouted. "What are you doing down there? Come on, we've been scared out of our minds looking for you. We need to get going. Come on, already."

Through the minimal light, she could barely make out that a body had been crouched deep into the mud and the muck. The head, as it stared back at her, began shaking.

"Spencer, it's enough already. Come on," she urged.

Again, the masked face shook no, unwilling to budge a single inch.

"Alright, prick. I've had it with you. I'm dragging you out of here."

Jenna reached her right arm into the space and began grabbing at the shadowy figure crouched just out of reach. She pressed her torso into the edge of the trailer, stretching her arm as far as she could, hoping he would take her hand and allow Jenna to pull him out of the muck. Jenna had more than enough of his shenanigans, and had grown furious.

"Spencer," she shouted. "Give me your fucking hand right now!"

She felt a hand grab hers. It tugged back slightly, before she pulled with all of her strength, lifting him up from between the two structures.

"You see, was that so ha—,"

Her voice cut out in an instant. Grasping her right hand, refusing to let go, was the left hand of a mysterious figure. His right hand, brandishing a rusty meat hook, slashed at her neck faster than a rattlesnake's strike. The point of the hook entered the left side of her neck, the force of the hit so strong, it cut clear through to the other side, slicing her trachea as it went. She clasped the gaping wound with both of her hands as she tried to scream for help. Blood gushed through her trembling fingers, spilling down her shirt all the way to her navel. As she took a few labored steps backwards, her feet slipped and slid through the messy, wet ground below. When she found some sense of footing, she locked her eyes on what she could only imagine was a monster come to life. In front of her, a colossal figure stepped out of the darkness, a thin moonbeam illuminating his stocky, awkward shaped body.

He was huge and towered over Jenna. His body, fat and pudgy, was covered in a leather smock coverall like a blacksmith might wear. The smock was splattered with blood, both fresh and old, and he reeked of death. He stood off kilter, his left shoulder hunched downward, and his head cocked to the side, draping downward towards his sloping left shoulder. It was as though he could not keep himself upright with his own power. Covering his head was Spencer's mask, dripping and smeared in crimson liquid.

He took a step towards her, followed by another. Whatever condition affected his shoulder and head, clearly made it uncomfortable to walk. As he moved his way towards her, the man let out a deep and painful grunt with every labored step. His right foot lifted from the ground as he stepped, his left foot dragged almost lifeless underneath his twisted and contorted body. Jenna spun her body and fell backwards against the wall of the middle trailer. Her hands were still grasping her throat which had been torn wide open. She gasped for air, unable to scream for help from her friends, or her over protective brother.

He moved in front of her and stared as the young, privileged life flooded out of her eyes. He dropped the meat hook onto the filthy floor and reached for something that leaned against the rusted wall. With both of his hands, he lifted an old gardening fork into the air and held it in front of a piggish belly that pushed the smock outwards. The wooden handle stretched 4-feet long and was equipped with 3 rusty metal prongs. He took a couple of deep, throaty breaths, lowered the gardening fork to his right, and shoved it deep into Jenna's abdomen. She dropped her hands from her throat, as blood and bile poured down her body like a dam that had been breached. With any bit of strength left within her spirit, she fought to remove the rusted prongs from her stomach, but she was too weak, and her blood, and life, was fading fast.

The man thrust the handle of the torture device towards the ground, and with loud groans, used the prongs inside Jenna's belly to lift her body up into the air. He pressed her hard against the wall and held her there, admiring the last fragments of light as they darkened in her eyes as she died slowly and painfully before him. Soon, gravity took over, and her body drifted downward, falling towards the ground. He pressed and held the forks firmly in place, stabbed into her abdomen. As she fell, the forks sliced her from stomach to rib cage, tearing the flesh from her bones. Ribbons of fresh, young skin piled up around the forks as her body came to rest against that wall. The man pulled back on the wooden handle, removing the spikes from her gut, as what was left of Jenna's body dropped like a loose anchor into the muddy ground below.

CHAPTER 11

Brad emerged from the darkness and trudged through the parking lot. It might have been the high, the booze - or both - but he found himself out of breath. It doesn't always matter how young or in shape you are, enough legal poison in your veins can slow anyone down.

"Lexi? Val? Jenna!" He shouted, his hands cupped around his mouth.

Lexi appeared from behind the convenience store and stepped over a half crushed cinder block wall surrounded by weeds. From the opposite side, out of the darkness, walked Val. They met him under the white light of the street lamps at the edge of the parking lot.

"Where the fuck is he?" Brad said with an angry tone, taking in quick breaths.

"And where is Jenna?" Lexi asked, looking around, surveying the scenery that wrapped them.

"Son of a *bitch*!" Brad shouted, taking a few steps forward into the sand. "Jenna! Spencer! Where are you?"

"Brad, wait," Lexi said through gasps, pointing at the trailers. "Right there, look!"

From behind the trailer closest to them, a figure stepped into view with its back facing them. The figure took a step, then another, as it stared into absolute nothingness. Then, even through the darkness, they noticed as the figure's head slowly shifted towards them. It now stared at the three teenagers from over its right shoulder. From their position, they were too far away to notice if there was any resemblance to Spencer or Jenna. There the figure stood, motionless for what seemed like a tremendous amount of time. Then the man took one step, followed by another labored step towards them.

"Who the fuck is that?" Val asked through fear and stuttered syllables.

"Spencer!" Brad shouted. "Quit fucking around, man. This isn't funny."

"What is this? Some sort of sick joke?" Lexi asked, looking at Brad. Her eyes dripped with anger. "Fuck this. I'm going to kick him in the nuts, just like *you* suggested. This is *not* funny."

With her fists clenched tight, she took off towards the mysterious man, purpose and fury in each of her steps. The figure continued to walk, or sort of drag himself through the sandy ground towards the 3 friends. His head drooped towards his left shoulder, and his upper body hung downwards as though his spine was snapped in two behind his ribcage. His right foot appeared to do all the work as he walked, his left foot appeared to be dragging behind him, leaving a jagged trail, as though it was drawing a shaky line in the sand. A rusted meat hook dangled from his right hand, swinging back and forth with his painful and forced steps. The mask adorning his head was off kilter, and was splattered with fresh blood. Lexi was so distracted by the anger that had built inside her, the words filling the surrounding air didn't register. Not at first. Not until the yelling became unmistakable. Brad was terrified. Regarding the man who now approached, they all should have been.

"Lexi," Brad shouted. His voice registering in Lexi's ears like a cymbal crash in an orchestra. "That's not Spencer!"

Lexi's eyes shoot open wider than the moon in the sky above as those words rattled around inside her skull. *Not Spencer.* She stopped dead in her tracks, watching as this unknown man continued to drag his pudgy body towards her. She took a few steps back before turning away from him. As she pressed her left foot into the dirt to kick-start her sprint back to Brad and Val - to safety - the man lifted his right arm, swinging that meat hook at Lexi. The pointy end just missed her lower back as her feet lifted out of the loose sand, propelling her body to what she imagined was help and security - Anything but what stood before her.

"Get to the car!" Brad shouted, his head peering over his left shoulder as he ran. "Lexi, come on! Run!"

Lexi ran as fast as her legs and asthma would allow. Brad was the first to reach the car, running around the back to reach the driver's door. Val shot open the back passenger door before diving in head first, landing face down onto the back seat. In one motion she pulled her feet and legs into the car, reaching for and slamming the door shut behind her. Brad tore the door open, jumped into the front seat and shuffled a set of keys in his hands. As his breath and heart raced inside his chest, he fumbled those keys for a moment before getting a grasp on them.

"Come on Lexi, come on Lexi," He muttered, repeatedly under his breath.

"We can't leave her out there," Val shouted, her hands on the back of Brad's seat. "Go get her!"

"She's coming, she's coming," He whispered, as he continued to gasp for air.

The passenger door shot open, as Lexi jumped in, landing hard on the passenger seat. She slammed the door shut behind her and pushed her long, blonde hair out of her face before turning to Brad.

"What the fuck are you waiting for?" She screamed, both hands in the air. "Let's get the fuck out of here!"

"We can't leave without Jenna and Spencer," Brad barked back.

"Then why did you tell us to get into the car?" Val screamed.

"I don't know! I don't, I didn't know what else to fucking do, OK?"

"Let's just go," Lexi said, clenching her teeth so tight, they could have crumbled to dust.

"OK, OK," Brad said through whispers. "Why the hell am I holding these keys? This car doesn't use a key!"

"Press the fucking button, stupid," Lexi yelled, reaching across the center console and slapping the ignition button.

"I'm scared, alright!" Brad screamed, both of his hands pressed against the sides of his head.

He pressed the ignition button. Nothing. The car wouldn't start. No sound came from the engine or the electrics inside the vehicle. Not even the slightest whimper.

"What the hell is happening," Brad said, confused.

He smacked the console with his open hand, then clenched his fist, punching it with every bit of strength he had.

"Why isn't it starting, Brad?" Lexi asked. Her voice trembled with a perfect mix of fear and fury.

"I," Brad stuttered. "I don't know."

"We can't just sit here and wait for this maniac to come for us," Val shouted as tears dripped down her smooth cheeks.

"We need to get back in that building. On the count of three, we all run as fast as we can to the back door. Got it?"

They all agreed. Brad began counting off, and as the word "three" rolled off his tongue, each door shot open with immense force, as Lexi, Val and Brad each hurried out of the useless vehicle. As each of their feet landed upon the pavement, without hesitation, they sprinted towards the crumbling old building. Before he could get past the trunk of the car, Brad slammed his feet into the blacktop to stop himself, flinging his body forward with enough force, he had to push his hands outward to keep from crashing into the asphalt. When he stood, in his right hand he held the charging wand. It had been removed from the port on the side of the Zeus X-1 and left on the ground. His brain did somersaults inside of his skull as he questioned everything happening to, and around them. He looked up from his right hand, still holding the lifeless, powerless wand as his eyes focused towards the darkness beyond the parking lot. There the figure stood, moonlight gleaming off the meat hook as he lifted it into the air, pointing it at Brad. He held it for a moment, then twisted his wrist so the spikey hook went from pointing at the ground to the sky above. The figure lifted it so that it was in line with his own throat, and he slowly slid it in front of his neck, as a warning gesture to the teenage boy. Brad gasped and swallowed the air hard, letting out a throaty gulp. He was mesmerized, struck in a trance of pure, unimaginable fear as their eyes locked. The figure dropped the hook to his side and took a large step forward. Brad couldn't move, terrified beyond the point of rational thought. Locked in by an invisible tractor beam spewing from the madman's eyes. Lexi's voice broke through the fog as her screams danced over his eardrums.

"Brad," she shouted, so hard that her voice shattered and her words quaked. "For fucks sake, Brad! Come on!"

Brad looked towards Lexi and Val, then back to the dark figure. As he approached, the smeared blood on his coveralls and Spencer's mask became more visible. Soon, the overhead lights of the tiny parking lot began to light the man, revealing more nightmare inducing visuals than even the bravest of souls could stomach. Brad dropped the charging wand, jumped to his right and burst into a full sprint as his feet landed in perfect sync on the fresh pavement.

Lexi and Val had climbed through the busted wall back to safety inside the crumbled structure. Val was through first, who reached her arms out into the cool, desert air, grabbing Lexi by the wrists to pull her inside. Once Lexi was in, Brad appeared. Wasting no time, he jumped over the metal shelving unit that had collapsed on the inside and slid down harshly. Once his feet hit the floor, he spun his body and with all the strength he could muster, lifted the shelf so that it blocked the makeshift entry way. He let go, allowing it to fall against the wall resulting in a loud thud. It shifted a bit to the side, screeching down the concrete walls before stopping and locking them inside.

"Who the hell is that?" Val shrieked, both hands covering her mouth as tears continued to flow down her face.

"How should I know?" Brad shot back.

Lexi, with her back against the far wall, sunk down so that she sat on the back of her heels. As she fell, she reached into her back pocket, retrieving her inhaler. Once her butt rested upon the backs of her legs and feet, she pressed the canister, inhaling three deep pumps from the device.

"Babe," Brad whispered as he knelt beside her. "Are you OK?"

Lexi nodded her head, staring directly in front of her, but at nothing at all. Her eyes were lost in a haze of fear and confusion. She looked up at Brad, and as their eyes met, he could see the horror deep inside of her soul. Lexi was tough, or so she pretended to be. And Brad had never seen his girlfriend like this. He wrapped his arms around her shoulders, pulling her in tight to his chest.

"We're going to be OK, babe," He whispered into her ear. He moved his right hand through her hair and down the back of her head. "We're going to be OK."

CHAPTER 12

Val paced back and forth across the filthy floor, so feverish that she could have burned a trail into the dusty, cracked concrete underneath her feet. Her left arm wrapped around her own waist, her right hand up to her mouth as her teeth nibbled and chewed her nails to the quick. Brad, shaken to the core, now sat cross legged, his right arm wrapped around Lexi as she sat with her legs pulled up to her chest. She rested her chin on her knees, her hands clasped together at her ankles. Each of them unaware of what the lunatic outside could be doing, or where he might be. Each of their minds and imaginations raced, figuring that the man was patiently waiting just outside to pick them off, one by one.

"Who could that be?" Val said through muffled speech as she chewed on her nails. "And what do they want from *us*?"

"How could we know that?" Brad asked with an attitude.

"It was rhetorical, dipshit," Val shot out. She stopped in her tracks, running both hands over her face before speaking again. "I'm, I'm sorry. I didn't mean that."

Brad shook off the apology. Truth was, he was just as scared as Valerie. If not more so. Even if he tried to hide it, the fear was rapidly bubbling to the surface.

"What should we do, Brad?" Lexi asked, staring up at him. "You sort of took charge as leader on this trip. Come on, think of something. We can't just sit here forever."

"What if we stayed inside and waited until morning? You know? Wait until the sun comes up, then get the car charging again and we can be on our way in no time. At least we could see that weirdo coming, right?"

"I guess," Lexi said, unsure of the proposal. "What do you think? The guy is some sort of vampire and he'll disappear when the sun comes up?"

"Haven't you ever seen any scary movies? Killers never come for you in the sunlight. They always kill at night. In the darkness. It adds to their, I don't know, fear factor."

"Fear factor?" Val asked, her words filled with judgment. "This isn't a scary movie, dude. This shit is *real*. And whoever that is, is *really* out there. Waiting for *us*. Besides, what about Jenna and Spencer?"

"When the car has a decent charge, we can get out of here and get to an area with an actual population. Then we can call the police and *they* can deal with that dude, and *they* will find Jenna and Spencer."

"We can't just leave Jenna and Spencer out there!" Val screamed. "What is wrong with you? That's your sister, your best friend. *My* best friend."

"Do you have any better ideas, Val?"

"Wait," Lexi said, shooting forward away from Brad. "The cops. That's what we can do. We can call the cops right now and tell them what's happening."

"Then we don't have to wait until sun up," Val added.

Lexi rose to her feet and began patting down each of her minimal pockets. All the hope in her face washed away as it turned a pale white.

"Where the hell is my phone?" She asked in a solemn tone, turning towards Brad.

Valerie checked her pockets only to be left with the same results as Lexi. Both of their phones were gone.

"I don't have mine, either," Val said.

"Brad, what's going on here?"

Brad jumped to his feet and took a few steps away from the girls until his back fell against the dirty, concrete wall.

"I don't," He stuttered. "I don't have either of your stupid phones."

"Then give me yours," Lexi said, her right hand outstretched.

"I don't have mine either."

"What do you mean, Brad? You don't have our phones, and you don't have your own? Our phones just went missing? Disappearing into thin air?"

"We left them in the car," Brad said, followed by a deep, nervous gulp. "They're in the car charging. Remember?"

Val and Lexi turned and their eyes met. Partially in disbelief, partially to see if the other's jaw had dropped to the floor.

"We were just in the car, and I didn't see any of our phones inside," Lexi said quietly.

"Whoever unplugged the car must have taken the phones, too," Brad declared.

Valerie placed both of her open palms on top of her head as she spun away from Brad. She walked across the room, and fell back into the path she had cut through the dust on the floor, chewing at her nails. Lexi's head cocked to one side, as her eyes squinted at Brad, burning holes through his body in disapproval.

"You dumb son of a bitch," Lexi said, shaking her head slowly. "What the hell are you trying to pull, huh?"

"What the hell kind of question is that?"

"You and your little shit stirrer friend planned this all along, didn't you?"

"Lexi," Brad said, his open palms held in front of his body, as though he may need to fight off an attack from his own girlfriend. "It's not what you think. I-I swear."

"Is that so," Lexi asked, as she began frothing at the mouth. "I think you and Spencer planned this entire thing just to scare us."

"Lexi, no."

"Yes Brad, yes. And I bet Jenna was in on it, too. Wasn't she? With her school girl crush on that dork."

Lexi took a few light steps in Brad's direction, seething at the idea her own boyfriend could be behind this disgusting display. She pushed in real close. So close, Brad could smell the anger as it poured from her body.

"That dude in the costume. That's Spencer, isn't it?"

"Lexi, I promise you. This isn't a joke."

"You're right, it's not," she said.

"Is that true?" Val asked. "Did you two set this up just to mess with us?"

"I'm telling the both of you, you've got this all wrong!" Brad was now shouting.

"Yeah, bullshit," Lexi said as she turned and made her way towards the metal shelf unit. "I'm going out there."

"Lexi, you can't!" Brad shouted.

Brad lunged at Lexi, grabbing her with both of his hands by the shoulders, pulling her body towards him. He spun her body and pushed her so hard that she fell to the ground, landing hard on her ass. In an instinctual move, Val shoved Brad with both her hands using all the strength she could pull out of her body.

"Don't you *dare* touch her!" Val shouted.

Brad tripped over some rubble on the floor, luckily catching his fall as he grabbed hold of an old snack display stand in the corner.

"You're a dick," Lexi said through deep breaths.

Lexi stood and dusted off her legs, glaring with the intensity of a thousand suns in Brad's direction. She motioned to Val, who covered Brad with a blanket of hate from her eyes. She walked with Lexi, keeping her eyes on Brad as she moved. Together, they could lift and move the metal shelf from the blown out opening on the back wall. They dropped the shelf to the ground where it shot dust up into the air and a screeching sound of twisted metal.

"I *am* going out there," Lexi said, staring at Brad in disgust. "I'm going to rip that mask off of Spencer's face, and then I will smack the taste out of his stupid mouth with it."

Lexi climbed up and through the opening to the outside world. When her feet met the sandy floor, she looked back at Brad.

"And just in case you didn't know this yet, *we're* through. Asshole."

"Lexi, wait!" Brad shouted as he jumped to his feet. He rushed to the exit, but before he reached it, Val moved into his path.

"You will *never* touch her like that again, you hear me? If you do, you won't need to worry about a masked maniac coming after you. I'll kill you myself."

Val stared into his soul as she climbed out after Lexi. Lexi had already walked around to the back of the building when Val's feet landed upon the dusty earth outside. Against his better judgment, Brad soon followed. He couldn't convince them that this wasn't part of some elaborate joke to scare the girls. And even if Lexi had just dumped him, he never wanted to see her hurt - or worse. Besides, their relationship was tumultuous, and this wasn't the first time those words had struck his ear drums. Lexi had declared them "being through" plenty of times in the past. And somehow, they always found their way back to one another. Teenage love - Always exciting, always toxic.

Lexi, with a generous head start, had made her way around the back of the building. She walked with what one could only imagine was false confidence. She was certain at this moment the man in the costume was Spencer doing everything he could to get a rise out of them.

"Hey Mr. Killer man," Lexi whispered, her hands cupped around her mouth. "Come out and get me, Mr. Scary desert guy. I'm *so* scared!"

Brad and Val crept their way around the back of the building, all the while keeping their distance from Lexi. She continued to coerce the man with taunting words.

"Lexi, please listen to me," Brad said in a panicked whisper.

"Brad, unless you want to see your plans go down in a ball of flames, I'd suggest you go back inside."

Just then, from the far end of the building, the man emerged. He turned to his right and stopped, gazing at them. They could hear him as he took in a load of deep breaths, his chest puffing frantically as his lungs expanded and burst with each breath through the rubber mask.

"Besides," Lexi said, turning back to the stranger now in front of her. "The girls can handle this themselves. We don't need you."

CHAPTER 13

There they stood for a long moment. Lexi, staring down at the masked figure where he stood at the far end of the building. A standoff, as though they were each about to remove a six-shooter from their hip at one another in a wild west duel. A tense yet playful smile washed over Lexi's face as she batted her eyelashes at him. The masked figure gave nothing back - no emotion or response of any kind. All they could see from the dim moonlight above was his pudgy stomach pushing the blood-soaked canvas coveralls outward, before moving back in as he took deep, gasping breaths. Valerie watched from afar, every passing second making her more afraid and unsure if Lexi was making the right call to action. Brad, who they no longer trusted, knew in his heart there was no chance Spencer was hiding underneath that blood splattered mask. Or was it? Had Spencer and Jenna come up with their own plan of attack? A plan to scare the daylights out of the rest of them? Some sort of sick joke before they left and made their way to Las Vegas? Brad had told everyone to make the most of it, and the mask Spencer wore was nothing, if not questionable and downright confusing. Maybe this was an act perpetrated by two love birds who had found a way to bond under the starry skies above. A strange bonding ritual, yes, but had he been wrong? He didn't know what to think as his mind and thoughts raced at full speed. All that was certain was that he was more scared than he had ever been in his brief life, and his girlfriend - or ex-girlfriend - was 30 feet away from revealing the truth. A truth he wasn't sure if he was ready to learn.

"So," Lexi said with a condescending giggle. She took a soft step forward. "You probably think you're pretty funny in that get up, don't you, *Spencer?*"

The masked man let out an audible grunt as his head tilted deeper to one side.

"We figured out your little joke, nerd boy," Lexi said, taking another couple of steps towards him. She continued to speak in an obvious, condescending tone. "Where's Jenna? Huh? Is she going to pop out at the most opportune time? Covered in *fake blood* to get us to jump and *pee* our *little pants?* Is that it, *Spencer?* Oh boy, I'm *so scared.*"

"Lexi," Brad shouted in a whisper. "Lexi, *please* stop. Please, come back inside."

"Look, Brad, honey," she said with a glance over her left shoulder. "If you're that scared, sweetie, go back inside where it's safe. Mm kay? Spencer and I have some talking to do."

She spun her gaze back to the man. Her head tilted down as she looked out through the tops of her eyes, the most obnoxious smile washing over her face. She took another couple steps forward.

"Now, Spencer," she said, letting out another tiny giggle. "This plan *might* have worked if Brad was a better actor. But, as you know - he's useless. He's *pathetic.* Just like you are."

The man lifted his chin towards the sky, letting out one, deep breath before his eyes landed again on Lexi.

"Spencer, I've had enough of this shit, OK sweetheart? Now, you've got *5 seconds* to take that *stupid* mask off, give yourself up and tell us where Jenna is. Or I will tear it off of your head and smack you so hard with it, I'll send you back in time. You hear me?"

The man let out another grunt while not breaking his intense stare. Lexi continued forward until they were within arm's reach of each other. She stared up at the man as he turned his head to the left, finally breaking eye contact. Lexi began counting down from 5.

"5…4…3…last chance honey," she said. "2…1!"

Lexi reached for and grabbed the top of the blood-spattered mask and ripped it off the man's head. Lexi held the mask up into the air as she smiled. She looked up at the mask, certain that when she shifted her eyes back at him, she would find a disgruntled and let down Spencer standing before her. The throaty gasps of Brad and Val behind her brought reality crashing hard onto her shoulders as she turned her head back to the man she had just unmasked.

Standing in front of her wasn't Spencer. Her eyes shot open at who - or what - she found. An older man one could guess was in his late 50s. His face was wrinkled and twisted as though it had been made of two men's faces that had at one time been sewn together to make one. His features were askew, and the right side of his face was littered with scars and tears from past stitches that never healed properly. Above his upper lip, a thick and disheveled mustache. His head tilted to one side involuntarily, as his eyes couldn't fix on any one thing at a time. Both of his eyes shot off into different directions, like hazy marbles that floated about independently inside of his skull. His cracked lips opened to reveal a toothless grin. The teeth that remained in his mouth were dark and rotting, apparent to them even in the dim light night sky.

Lexi tried to choke out a scream, but nothing would come out of her throat, and her body couldn't move. She was frozen. Petrified by the man standing before her. It was a living embodiment of every nightmare anyone ever had, accumulated into one living, breathing monster of a man.

"Lexi," Brad whispered, like he was coercing a dog that had run out of the house. "Lexi, get back here. Come on, babe. Come back to me. Please. Come here Lexi!"

She remained there, frozen stiff in pure terror. Enough fear now flowed within her veins, clouding any chance of rational thinking. Her bottom lip quivered, her eyes turned to glass and her knees shook so heavily that they knocked into one another. Brad's incessant begging couldn't break through the shock that now occupied her mind. She watched as this devilish man lifted his right hand to his face, holding that rusty old meat hook. His eyes bounced around in his head as he attempted to focus on the sharp point of the hook. So much so, that his eyes continued to flick back and forth, almost like he was giving each eye a turn to focus on the object. Each eye danced between staring through her and watching the cold steel hang in the cool, breezy air.

The man held the hook outward as a disgusting smile broke out on his face. He twisted the hook in front of him, reveling and smiling at it as it twirled. After a moment that seemed to last an eternity in Lexi's shocked state, he stopped it and held it perfectly still. Somehow, both of his swimming eyes focused on Lexi. The smile washed away in an instant and transformed into a scowl. As he lowered the hook to his chest, he spoke to her in a throaty, phlegm filled voice.

"Run," He grunted.

Brad grabbed Valerie by the waist as he turned and took off in a full, panicked sprint towards the back of the building. Valerie followed his lead, hoping they could get inside the building before this man, who appeared half-crippled, could get to them. The man's voice shook Lexi out of her stupor, as she shook her head a few times, landing back in this unfortunate reality. A reality no one would ever want to witness. A reality no one could ever believe.

She turned and dashed into the desert, running faster than her legs had ever allowed straight ahead into the unknown darkness. As Brad hoisted Valerie through the blown-out hole in the building, he looked to his right to see Lexi explode like a bolt of lightning into the darkness, soon becoming nothing more than a shadow. Nothing short of a memory.

"Lexi, No!" He screamed. So loud, it could have shaken the foundation of the old building.

He held Valerie by the waist, ushering her inside. Once her feet hit the concrete floor, Brad turned to chase after his girlfriend. As he approached the edge of the building, he jumped back with all of his might as the rusty hook swung past his torso. It crashed into the side of the building, sending chipped concrete and dust into the air. As the man emerged from the shadows, he stood face to face with Brad. The man's mouth, again, boasted a mile-wide smile, as his sticky and discolored tongue began licking his cracked, dry lips. As he tore the hook from the wall, Brad turned and jumped through the hole in the brick wall, diving head first inside the building. Without saying a word, he and Valerie lifted the metal shelving unit and placed it over the hole, erasing any chance of the man - or Lexi - getting inside.

Lexi ran and ran faster than she knew she could, and farther into the remote landscape than she ever should. As she ran, she turned her head just enough over her left shoulder to see how close this maniac might be. As she looked, her right foot kicked a rock that was buried deep into the sand. She let out a loud gasp as she crashed into the desert floor. Landing upon her chest so hard, that her legs bent the entirely wrong way over her back, as her face sunk deep into the dirt. She pressed her hands into the sand, lifted her body and continued to run. In such a panic, she didn't realize, thanks to the hard spill, that her inhaler had been tossed from her pocket and remained behind.

She continued running, unsure of what she was hoping to find. Safety? There wasn't a soul for miles aside from her friends and the maniac. A maniac, who, for all they could imagine, wanted nothing more than to rip their souls from their bodies and tear the energy, love and hope from each one. She ran until suddenly, the ground from beneath her feet disappeared. For a split second, her body remained suspended in midair, until she crashed, face first, into a wall of slimy, sticky dirt.

She slid down the wall landing flat on her back in a pool of sticky liquid. She splashed around while gasping for air, digging her hands deep into the muck, pushing herself up to her feet.

The surrounding air reeked and as her brain attempted to distinguish all the wretched smells surrounding her, she choked on the sour, putrid air and gagged uncontrollably. The air, as well as the muck that now covered her body, created an awful mélange of excrement, rotting flesh and the slightest hint of gasoline. She stepped through the ankle-deep mess to the dirt wall. She began clawing at the dirt, hoping to pull herself out of this pit from hell she was unfortunate enough to find. The wretched stench burned her lungs and throat, as an asthma attack overtook her body. She gasped for air, both hands pressed hard into her chest, as furious and violent coughs made her body convulse. She reached for her pockets to retrieve her inhaler hoping to catch her breath.

"Oh no," she whispered through an intense coughing fit. "My inhaler. No, no!"

She grew even more frantic as she realized her inhaler was gone. Gasping for air, she held her throat as the rancid air burned her lungs, nose and mouth. Involuntarily, her body rejected the air, as she coughed and choked on bile that raced up her throat.

From the moonlight above, it illuminated the deep hole enough for her to notice she had fallen into some sort of burn pit. That much she knew. What was burned within the pit, she didn't want to know. To her left she could almost make out what appeared to be a ravaged rib cage sitting next to a crushed human skull.

"Help!" She screamed until her voice gave out. "Brad! Someone! *Please* fucking help me! Get me out of here! Brad, please!"

As she continued to claw at the loose dirt, scratching to reach the lip of the pit and pull herself to safety, she saw a shadow appear and loom over her. The shadow crept in like a fever, blacking out any moonlight that allowed her vision to focus. She stepped back through the sticky, thick liquid covering her feet and watched as the shadow lifted its right arm into the air. The sound of metal clicking filled the air, followed by a deep scratch of steel. A blast of tiny sparks lifted into the air, followed by the dance of a single flame. The maniac held the flame as it danced side to side in the breeze just in front of his face, illuminating his rotting smile as his two lazy eyes floated aimlessly trying to focus on her. In his hand, he held Spencer's Zippo lighter. He pushed his hand out and over the pit and let go, and the lighter began its slow descent into the pit with Lexi.

"No, No! NO!" Lexi screamed, as time fell into slow motion.

She jumped away from him, slamming her back into the wall of dirt, as the burn pit engulfed in raging flames. Lexi screamed - screams that only the evilest of demons could dream. As the flames ripped through her clothes, her flesh burned as it melted from her bones. The man watched, his shoulder ticking up and down as he laughed at Lexi burning alive in front of him. Soon, her screams died as her body fell into the sea of flames.

The man, lit up from the bright blaze before him, lifted the blood-soaked mask he stole from Spencer and placed it onto his head yet again. He turned his head the best he could, as he directed his devilish stare back at that old building. For him, the night was young, and there was more work to be done.

CHAPTER 14

"Wait," Valerie shouted as they lifted the metal shelf to close the entryway to the building. "Brad, wait! Lexi is still out there. We have to go get her!"

"Are you kidding me?" Brad asked, his eyes as wide as two globes in fear. "Help me lift this damn shelf. That *monster* is right outside."

"What about Lexi, Brad? We can't leave her out there with him!"

"He almost killed me!" Brad barked, spit shooting from his mouth as he screamed. "Come on, we need to keep him out there. We need to save ourselves."

Valerie shook her head in disapproval, but knew there was no time to argue. She grabbed one end of the heavy blockade, and with Brad's help, forced it into place the best she could. Once it was set and covered any way in - or out - Valerie walked away from him. She paced the floor, running her trembling hands over her face and head in frantic motions.

"I can't believe you left her out there to die!"

"What was I supposed to do, Val?" He shouted. "He swung that fucking, *hook*, thing at me. Almost cut me right open. Besides, I didn't see you trying to save her."

"How dare you blame this on me!" Val shouted. She rushed to Brad and grabbed him by the shoulders as she screamed in his face. "That's *your* girlfriend, you asshole! And you, not me, *you* left her to die."

"She ran into the desert! What was I supposed to do?"

Val let go of him and walked to the other side of the room. Tears poured down her soft cheeks as she covered her mouth with her right hand. Her left, planted on her left hip. She gasped for air through the tears to speak. She was scared, angry and felt like she could go into shock.

"Well, we have to do something," she said as her voice trembled.

"We need a plan."

Brad rushed past Valerie into the front room of the long-forgotten store. He began frantically looking around, overturning dusty, sun-drenched displays, half-broken chairs and other items that had been left behind long ago.

"What are you doing?" She asked.

"There has to be something here. Something that can be used as a weapon. I don't know."

"You're going to fight that maniac? Did you see him? He looked like something brought to life out of the book of Revelations. He looked like he spawned from hell."

"Well what ideas do you have, huh?" He screamed, throwing a rock he had found against the wall with all his might.

"Brad, calm down. We need to think this through."

"What is your plan? Huh? Hide in here for the rest of eternity. That won't work, Val. That fucking maniac will get in here and kill us, eventually. He's probably looking for a way in right now."

Just then, their conversation, or screaming match, was interrupted by an eerie sound. A sound that pierced their eardrums like that of long, thick nails on an old, filthy chalkboard. They both covered their ears with their hands and closed their eyes, hoping if they couldn't see anything, maybe they wouldn't hear it, either.

"Oh my god, what is happening?" Val shouted.

"I don't know," Brad screamed. "What is that sound?"

From the inside, they could see a large shadow walk slowly past one of the dusty, filth covered windows. As the shadow passed, the maniac sunk his meat hook into the dirty glass, dragging it in a jagged motion from one side to the other. Then, slamming it into the next window, filling the air with that dreadful sound. He walked around the building, taunting them from the outside.

Valerie, with her ears covered, backed into the far wall as her knees buckled and she crashed to the ground, blurting out a scream that could have awakened the dead. Brad ducked behind what was once the register counter, both of his hands clasped tight over his ears to block the horrid sound from outside.

"Leave us alone!" Valerie screamed. "What do you want from us you crazy mother fucker!"

"Wait!" Brad screamed.

Valerie looked over just as he shot up from behind the counter.

"I've got it!" He shouted, as he swung a wooden baseball bat over his head, sending it crashing to the counter top. Dust and particles flipped and swirled in the air. "This will do," He said. "It will *have* to do."

CHAPTER 15

A brand new, beautiful Lincoln Town car made its way up the driveway to the Miller family home, stopping next to Lexi's sparkling BMW. As it sat in the driveway, the gorgeous Bay Area sun hit and bounced off the waxed and washed body of the luxury automobile. As the engine shut off, the driver side door flung open, making way for a man to exit. He wore a full black, perfectly tailored suit that had been recently pressed. He was tall, clean-shaven and wore a black driver's cap which covered his shaved haircut. As he stepped out, he brushed the suit jacket before reaching for the back driver side door.

"Here we are, Mr. and Mrs. Miller," The man said, almost toneless.

One foot, followed by another, each adorned with expensive dress shoes stepped onto the driveway. It was Mr. Miller, Brad and Jenna's father. He wore a pair of khaki pants, with a short sleeved white shirt covered in sky blue stripes that was tucked in. A matching blue sweater was tied around his shoulders, flowing down his back. He had striking blue eyes and blonde hair with gray highlights. His hair was long and flowed down his neck with the perfect amount of poof to it, and his hairline was pushed way back on his forehead. He stood up straight, stretched his lower back and reached into the back seat to assist his wife in exiting the car.

"Thank you, Stephen," Mr. Miller said to the driver without looking at him.

Mr. Miller's hand emerged from the vehicle with a smaller hand clasped inside. The hand had long, red painted nails, clearly done professionally and of course cost a fortune.

Mrs. Miller allowed her husband to pull her up and out of the back seat. She stood on the driveway wearing a pair of long, white pants that draped over her open-toed high heel shoes. On top, she wore a silk, blue shirt tied into a knot at her navel. Her dark blonde hair was pulled back into a well-manicured ponytail, and perfectly cut bangs cascaded down her forehead towards her striking eyes. Not a single hair was out of place on either of their heads. That wouldn't be allowed, not for the Millers. She tossed an oversized - and overpriced - handbag over her left shoulder as she scoffed at the driver and walked towards the house.

"Please bring the bags inside, Stephen," Mr. Miller said, handing him a wad of cash. "Just leave them in the foyer, we will take care of it from there."

"Yes, sir," Stephen said, tucking the cash into the inside pocket of his suit jacket.

As the Millers reached the front door, Mr. Miller stuck the key in, unlocking first the deadbolt, followed by the door handle.

"Look, hun," He said. "I know you're upset our vacation was canceled. But you don't need to be rude to the driver."

"Just get the door open, Thomas," she replied with a disappointed sigh. "I need a long bath before we plan a makeup vacation."

"Makeup vacation?" He asked with a small giggle, pushing the front door wide open.

"Yes, a makeup vacation," she said, pushing past him. "You still owe me a vacation. And don't you forget it."

She leaned in and gave him a soft, passionate kiss. She followed the kiss with a playful slap on her husband's cheek.

The foyer of the Miller's home was impeccable. Brightly colored imported Italian tile stretched as far as the eye could see throughout the home. To the left, a massive staircase that curved as it went, creating a sexy aesthetic leading to the second floor of the home. A crystal chandelier hung in the middle of the room, sending beautiful, sparkling rainbows throughout the entire space. An expensive and ornate rug sat at the base of the stairs. To the right, an antique wooden table with a stone planter on top bursting at the seams with fresh-cut flowers, resulting in a beautiful and fresh scent throughout the front of the home.

"If you need me, I'll be in a hot bath with a glass of wine. While *you* plan a new vacation."

He shook his head, letting out another giggle when his head shifted, allowing his eyes to land upon the driveway. He squinted, noticing that something wasn't right. Something was off.

"Honey," He shouted into the house.

"Yes, dear," she yelled from the top of the stairs. Her voice fluttered with the perfect level of condescension that came off as almost flirty.

"Uh, weird question. Where the *fuck* is my brand-new Zeus?"

"What do you mean?" She asked as she walked back down the stairs.

She moved across the massive front room to meet her husband, twisting and looking around the open door towards the area that would otherwise be the resting spot for the Zeus X-1.

"Is it in the garage?" She asked.

"No. You made sure I left the garage open for the Jaguar and the Range Rover. Remember?"

"And who's BMW is that?"

Mr. Miller's eyes shot wide open as his brain caught up with the situation.

"God damn that kid," He screamed, reaching for his phone. "That's Lexi's car. Brad took my Zeus."

"Aren't the kids going to Las Vegas this weekend for that big concert, or festival? Whatever the hell it is?" Mrs. Miller asked.

"Yes," He said through clenched teeth. "Yes, they are."

He flicked through the contacts on his cell phone, slammed his index finger into the screen and pressed it close to his right ear.

"I'm telling you this much," He said, looking at his wife. His eyes filled with intense rage. "If he isn't dead in a ditch somewhere. Trust me. I'll kill him myself."

CHAPTER 16

Thomas Miller walked out the front door of his home when he heard the police car roll into the driveway. In a pair of loose-fitting white cloth pants and a thin white button-up shirt that appeared two sizes too big, Mr. Miller was floating through the air more than walking. The shirt was unbuttoned down to the middle of his chest, and he wore a pair of large aviator sunglasses. As the police officer opened the car door, Mr. Miller was slamming the front door to the house with intensity. The cop knew then - This wouldn't be a fun interaction.

"Good afternoon, Sir. I'm Officer Pullman," He said as he walked around the back of his cruiser.

"Thomas. Thomas Miller," Mr. Miller said in a low, uninterested tone. "Took you long enough to get here, huh?"

"Well Mr. Miller, this is a big city that we have to monitor. But, I apologize for the delay. If there was one."

"You know, if elected leaders would step up and do their jobs, you and your fellow officer's lives might be easier."

"We do what we can, Sir," The officer said with a fake smile. He reached into his front, left shirt pocket removing a small pad of paper and a pen. "So, what can I do for you today, sir?"

"Alright, where to begin," Mr. Miller said, removing his sunglasses. He didn't make eye contact with the officer, instead, he gazed off at the horizon, keeping his eyes locked on the view over the entire city. Mr.

Miller would swear on a bible that he supported the police and first responders. But if he were to look deep within himself, he knew - and it was obvious - Mr. Miller felt he was above any blue-collar worker or civil servant. They were there to serve him, and he never missed an opportunity to express that sentiment.

"It would appear that my smart-ass son has taken one of my cars without my knowledge or permission."

"So, a car is missing?"

"Isn't that what I just said? Yes, my car is missing."

"And you're certain your son took this car? There is no chance anyone else stole or took it?"

"I don't think that's my job to figure out, Officer. That's why I called you."

"OK," Officer Pullman's patience was waning. "What makes you believe it was your son? How old is he and what's his name?"

"His name is Brad, and he will be 18 soon. He went to Vegas for the weekend with his sister and a couple of their idiot friends. Some stupid music festival or something. I don't even know. I don't even care. I just want that car back."

"Forgive me for asking," Officer Pullman knew this might set off a stick of human dynamite. "Have you tried calling your son?"

"No answer. Him or his sister."

"And have you reached out to the other parents?"

"Again, wouldn't that be *your* job?"

"Uh, well. We can reach out to the parents. But, it might be helpful for you to speak directly with them. If they have any information, they could share it—"

"OK Look," Mr. Miller shot out, turning to face the officer. "The car is a Zeus X-1. It's black and I have the license plate written down for you." Mr. Miller handed the officer a folded piece of paper pulled from his shirt pocket. "I'd like to report it as stolen."

"So, you want to proceed with this case as a stolen car? Even if your son and his friends do have it?"

"You got it," Mr. Miller said as he leaned against the back of the police cruiser, a large, smug smile now washed over his face.

"You understand your son, daughter and their friends will be arrested for this, correct? They could end up with a felony on each of their records for car theft."

"I understand the consequences, they're the ones that need this speech. Not me. But thank you. Each of them should have thought about this before they took my car."

The officer's eyes widened in surprise at the cold-hearted words spewing from Mr. Miller's mouth. He looked at the slip of paper and slid it into his uniform pocket.

"OK, I'll proceed with this report as a stolen car," He said, shock and awe still consuming his mind. "And you said they went to Las Vegas, huh?"

"Right. But the car can only go so far on a single charge. So, I know they would've had to stop somewhere along the way to charge it. I just hope that moron doesn't destroy that car. My god. He better not destroy that car."

"If you provide me with your son or daughter's cell numbers, or the numbers of their friends, we can trace them and see which tower they're pinging. Or at least the last tower they were near. That will give us a good idea of where they could be."

"Sounds good to me. Both their numbers are on that slip I gave you," Mr. Miller said, putting his sunglasses back on his face. "Do your worst, huh?" He patted the officer twice on his right shoulder. He walked back towards the front door of his home.

"We'll do what we can, sir. When we have any information, we'll call you. Hopefully we find them soon and that they're OK."

"Yeah," Mr. Miller said in a drawn-out tone, turning back to face the officer. "I'm sure they're fine. Just focus on finding the car, yeah? You do your job as a cop, I'll do my job as the parent."

CHAPTER 17

Brad sat at the far corner of the room trembling, his back against the wall and his legs curled into his body. His knees pointed up to the crumbling ceiling, each of his wrists resting on them while he twiddled his fingers. His eyes darted around the room, almost as though he hoped he might be dreaming. A nightmare come to life for him, his sister and their friends that, at any moment, maybe he would wake up. Anguish flooded from his pores, creating an invisible haze of horror around him that encapsulated the entire room. Much more visible was the sweat that had gathered on his brow dripping down his face. Sweat stains had also grown, dried and resurfaced on his clothing. With his left hand, he grabbed his right, pinching down tightly on the skin between his thumb and index finger. He closed his eyes tight while he pinched down harder and harder until the pain became too much to bear. He opened his eyes, clunked his head against the wall and stared at the ceiling. Hoping that a deep, painful pinch might wake him from this hell. That is what everyone says, right? Unfortunately, this nightmare was all too real. He focused his eyes on Valerie.

Valerie paced the room, continuing to cut a path with her feet as she walked back and forth. Her hands were cupped together, pressed into her chest with a long strand of beads that fell down both of her wrists. While she paced, she continuously muttered something to herself under her breath. She whispered so soft, that Brad could not hear what she was saying. He watched from afar, attempting to make out the words she was whispering to herself.

"Hey," Brad spoke to break the silence. "What are you saying to yourself?"

Valerie stopped in her tracks, shooting an angry look at Brad over her right shoulder. She glared down at him before she closed her eyes and began pacing and muttering again.

"Hey, Valerie."

"Shut up, Brad," she said, not opening her eyes and returning to her whispers.

"Look, we need to work together here. It's the only way we're going to get out of this."

This time, Valerie didn't look at Brad. She didn't even acknowledge his words. He continued watching her as she went until he gathered the courage to attempt gaining her attention again.

"Val, come on. Talk to me—"

"Shut the *fuck up* Brad!" She shouted, planting her feet into the concrete floor while pounding her fists into her hips.

"Whoa, Val—"

"No," she said with her eyes closed while shaking her head. "You don't call me that. We're not friends. Not anymore."

"What the hell does that mean?"

"Are you kidding me?" She asked, her eyes half-shut in disgust, glaring over her right shoulder. "How could you think we're friends?"

"You came on this fucking trip, didn't you?"

"Yes!" She shouted, her fists again pounding into her thighs. "I came on this trip to hang out with Jenna. Your *sister*. You think if I even half expected this nightmare to happen that I would have come? That I would be stuck in this situation? With *you* of all people?"

"Problem is, *Valerie*, this nightmare *has* occurred. And we all need to stick together to make it out," He said as he stood to his feet.

"Stick together?" She asked in a mocking tone. "Is that why you left Lexi out there alone? Is that why your best friend *and* your sister are nowhere to be found? Was that sticking together, Brad?"

"Hey, we did what we had to do. You were out there, you saw what happened."

"What exactly happened? In your words. In your mind, that is."

"I tried to get Lexi to come back to us. You heard me. I was screaming at her to come back. I didn't tell her to run into the fucking desert alone."

Valerie glared at him in disgust for a moment before winding back with her right arm, swinging it across her body and smacking him clean across his face. He recoiled and pressed his left hand to his cheek. He lifted his head as their eyes met, as he let out a short, nervous giggle and took a step away from her.

"OK," He said, nodding his head. "I guess I deserved that a bit."

"A bit? Please. You deserved that one, and many more."

"Well," Brad said with a chuckle. He turned and walked back to the other side of the room where a once bustling register and counter had sat. He pressed his hands onto the top of the filthy counter and lifted his head to Valerie. "I don't know about all that."

Brad lifted and looked at his palms to see the excessive level of dust that gathered onto them thanks to a breached dam of sweat that had pooled within them. Without much thought, he wiped his palms on his athletic shorts.

"I tried to save her," He said, very sure of himself. "But now I *can* save us. Valerie, come on, work with me here. You've got to trust me."

"Trust you? I don't trust you and you know that," she said with her teeth clenched tight. "To be quite honest, if I wasn't sure this maniac would kill me on sight, I might trust him more than I do you."

"Well that's just harsh, Val."

"Don't call me Val, asshole."

"What is your fucking problem with me, exactly?" He snapped, throwing his hands in the air.

"Do you not remember last year?"

"Oh god. Here we go," He said, shaking his head with a healthy eye roll.

"Fuck you, with your 'here we go'," she shouted. She bent down, picking up an empty, rusted oil can. She wound up and tossed it at him as hard as she could, just missing as it passed his head and crashed into the wall behind him. "You don't remember last summer? Because I sure do."

"No, no," He said, rubbing the back of his head, refusing to look up at Val. "I remember. I remember everything."

"So you remember making out with me at that rich girl, Brianne's party? You know, the one? The one where you pissed off Lexi so bad, she left early?"

"Yes, Valerie, I remember what happened. OK?" He barked as he turned his back to her. "I thought we were well past this bullshit."

"Oh well," She shouted as she flailed her arms throughout the air in a very pronounced, exaggerated way. "You thought we were fine. So, shit, I guess it's all water under the bridge."

"Yes, I thought it was."

"Brad, you fed me drinks *all* night. Once I was plenty drunk, you made out with me and told me you had always been into me," she yelled. "You told me you were going to leave Lexi and be with *me*. And somehow I was stupid enough to believe you."

"I was drunk, too," He barked back, swiping his right hand across the dusty counter as he went.

"What's new?" She asked, crossing her arms across her chest. "Every weekend, every party, shit, every chance you get. You're drunk."

"Low blow, Val."

"Is it, Brad? Or is it a low blow to make out with a drunk girl who is younger than you and tell her how you're going to leave your girlfriend for her? Huh? And let me ask you this, did you ever tell Lexi about us? About what happened?"

"Of course not," He said with a stern, matter-of-fact tone.

"Do you realize how awkward this has always been for me? I mean, I have to see you with her knowing what you did. What *we* did. I should have told her."

"No, absolutely not," He said, almost as though he was begging her not to. "She would kill both of us if she found out."

"That probably doesn't matter, now. You left her out there with that masked maniac. God only knows what he's done to her. Or to Spencer and Jenna," she said. She turned and burned a hole into his face with her eyes. "You don't deserve her, Brad. You don't deserve any quality girl. You're an asshole."

"Yes, you're right," He shouted. "I was a fucking dick. I have *always* been a jerk. I know that. And I apologized for what happened - What I did and said to you. And I am still so sorry."

He rushed around the counter towards Valerie. She took a few steps back trying to get away from him, but the clutter and mess covering the floor made that more difficult than she imagined. He grabbed at her shoulders as she tried to fight him off. She flailed her arms in his face, smacking him and hitting him numerous times. Finally, he caught both of her wrists in a soft grasp. He wasn't trying to hurt her. Just, in his mind, hoping to reason with her.

"Val, stop! Look at me!"

She shook her head as tears flooded down her cheeks. All of this had become way too much for the human mind to endure.

"Please, Val," He begged. "Just look at me. Listen to me."

She softened the muscles in her arms and shoulders as the two made eye contact with one another.

"Val, I am so sorry," He said with as much sincerity as he had ever been able to muster. "Please. Forgive me. I'm sorry I hurt you. I promise, I'll never hurt you again, and I will never allow anyone else to hurt you either."

She could see the sincerity in his eyes, and the tears slowed. She nodded her head and wiped her nose with the right arm of her sweatshirt.

"I'm so sorry, Val," He repeated. "I promise, I'll always be here for you. And I will spend every day trying to show you and Lexi that I can be a good guy. A good friend."

"OK, Brad," she said, wiping her nose yet again.

"Come here," He whispered, wrapping his arms around her shoulders.

She folded into his chest and let out a deep sigh. This wasn't love blooming or the flame of lust igniting. This was more so proof someone could change for the better. Even under their current circumstances, that meant the world to Valerie.

"Now, we need to stick together. That is the only way we can make it out of this mess."

"What are we going to do?" She asked. "We need some sort of plan."

"Well, we can't just sit in here all night. He knows we're here. He could come for us at any time. Besides, if we sit and wait for the sun to come up, who knows what could happen to Spencer, Jenna and Lexi."

"So what do we do?"

"I've got it," He shouted.

Brad rushed through the rubble back to the counter. He ducked below and began throwing miscellaneous items around the room.

"I think we need to take this son of a bitch head on."

"How? Did you see that hook he had? We can't fight him. Besides, he's huge."

"I'm an All State track star, Val. I have kicked the ass of many dudes bigger than him."

"Brad, come on," she said with a sideways stare. "If you're going to change, being honest would be a good start."

"OK, fine," He caved. "Maybe I haven't. But I know I could. You know, if I had to."

"And how do you expect to beat him? He has weapons. We don't."

Brad lifted his right arm above his head, brandishing that same wooden baseball bat. He swung it down so that it crashed loudly onto the counter top. Dust and debris kicked up into the air like a million dandelion spores.

"With this."

CHAPTER 18

A year earlier…

In the dinghy hallway just outside the dining room of Captain Kairo's Fish House, Valerie sat alone. A line of 6 banquet chairs had been placed in the hallway, each one in a different, although all too similar state of decay with their chipping silver legs and ages old floral print that graced both the seat and back. She chose the second chair from the left in a calculated attempt to keep anyone from joining her. She felt if she had sat closer to the middle, it would seem inviting or welcoming to a passerby or witness. If she was off center, maybe her position would seem askew enough that it would appear as though she was only taking a mild break, and less like a much needed escape from not only other guests, but all of reality as she now knew it.

Her long, flowing black hair had been pulled over the top of her head and now cascaded over her forehead and face as her eyes faced the rotting carpet underneath her. Her perfectly pressed black dress, with big poofs at the shoulders was chosen by her mother. Against her own wishes, she wore it, but only because she didn't want to disappoint her. Especially not today of all days. So reluctantly, she put the damn thing on. Underneath, she wore black leggings that disappeared into a pair of black flats. Her hands were cupped at her knees as her right leg continuously bounced up and down, showcasing her apparent anxiety to the room.

Captain Kairo's had long been one of her father's favorite restaurants. Though the decor - both inside and out - had seen better days and years, the food, in his words, was "Exceptional." The floral print carpeting that stretched throughout the entire place was stained and unclean, which, of course, matched the chairs perfectly. Almost as though the designer had unearthed a surplus of yellow background print, covered in red and green flowers and somehow found a carpet to pair. Clearly, a design choice was made, for better or worse. The walls of the restaurant were made of faux wood siding and meant to resemble a fisherman's shack, decorated with various nets, mounted fish and photographs of regulars and their catch of the day. There were also many old nautical maps of San Francisco for good measure gracing the walls. Deteriorating wooden tables and booths fashioned with crimson vinyl wrapped the dining room, and the dim lighting was made to seem that much darker thanks to the red glass bowls that covered each of the lightbulbs. Captain Kairo's was a dock workers hangout if there ever was one.

Valerie's father, Hector Gutierrez had worked on one of the many docks on San Francisco bay. He ran a crew of folks who loaded and unloaded boats each and every long, hard and cold day on the San Francisco shore. One morning, a new trainee was running the forklift while attempting to unload shipping crates that had arrived at the dock. The cargo ship carried containers of various items that had come in to supply different restaurants, stores and other locations around the sprawling city. The young worker had grown cocky and thought too highly of himself after a couple successful trips to and from the cargo boat that had docked at the pier. On what was to be his last run, with that new streak of cockiness flowing through his blood stream, he pressed up the ramp at too high a rate of speed, causing the forklift to slide off the right side. The ramp caught the machine from the bottom and held it momentarily, causing the worker to spiral into an understandable panic. That is when Hector jumped in, as well as some of the other veteran employees.

Hector rushed to his aide, standing on the ramp and reaching for the young man to pull him to safety. Hector yelled to *'Forget the forklift and packages, just grab my hand!*' But the boy, in a state of terrible fear, couldn't hear what he was saying. Maybe it was that he couldn't hear him, maybe it was that he just didn't listen. Regardless, the young man dove from the forklift into the frigid waters below, and in doing so, the forklift toppled towards the water along with him. As the cabin, the heaviest portion of the lift, slipped from the ramp and began its descent into the water, the fork turned in a violent motion towards Hector. Before he could move out of harm's way, the left fork twisted at the weight of the vehicle and connected with the side of Hector's head, sending him to the water, unconscious.

When they pulled him from the water, he was already dead. In fact, they figured that the blunt force may have killed him instantly. Valerie always found it, odd if nothing else, maybe even bordering on heartless, the fact the Doctors told the family this. As though it was some sort of consolation prize that he didn't suffer.

When a spouse and parent dies, many things die with them. Love, comfort, familiarity and as Valerie had learned, even a little part of you dies. Valerie's mother had been a champion throughout all of this. She had to be, for the sake of the three kids. 7-year-old Maria, 12-year-old Silvio and Valerie, at the time, 16-years-old. And the day they had dreaded most of all since the accident had arrived. Today was the funeral and celebration of life. And where else to celebrate Hector's life than his favorite restaurant surrounded by his favorite people and favorite thing of all - The sea.

Family members from all over had traveled to say their last goodbyes and pay their final respects to the man they once knew, still loved and would always remember. Cousins, aunts - both distant and otherwise - as well as friends and co-workers all gathered to enjoy the food and ambiance Hector spoke so highly of. Different buffet dishes filled with coconut shrimp, cajun sea bass, fried cod and crab legs remained warm and edible underneath heat lamps. But Valerie had seen and heard enough. She could only take so many hugs and had grown sick of having to hear how sorry everyone was for her loss. For once, she just wanted to be alone in her thoughts and her sadness.

Across the room, standing arm's length away from the bar was Valerie's longtime best friend, Jenna. Wearing a long-sleeved black dress with a popped white collar that folded down her neck. Her hair was done in pigtails, looking like the spitting image of Wednesday Addams. She had been standing by the bar waiting and hoping for one of the adults to look away long enough that she could sneak their drink from the bar top and enjoy it without being carded. When the overweight man on one of the creaking barstools turned his back, Jenna snagged the rocks glass filled with alcohol and a juice mixer. She didn't know what it was and didn't care. If it got her buzzed, then her mission was complete.

As she turned from the bar, she lifted the glass to her lips and took a deep sip from the cocktail straw that stuck out of the drink. As she sipped, her eyes landed upon Valerie sitting in the hallway, alone. She could feel her heart sink for her best friend. She turned back to the bar and noticed another freshly poured cocktail had been left unattended and snapped it up in her other hand. Walking as though she owned the place, she made her way towards Valerie with the strong drinks.

"Is this seat taken?" Jenna asked, motioning at the empty seat to Valerie's left.

"Huh?" Valerie replied, brushing the hair from her face to look at who had approached her. "Oh, no. Sorry. Go ahead."

"Here, I brought you this," Jenna said, handing Valerie the mystery drink. She plopped herself down onto the chair so hard the legs shrieked.

"Thanks. What is it?"

"Does it even matter?" Jenna asked with a laugh, taking another sip of her cocktail. "I know they won't serve us. So I took matters into my own hands. I figured if anyone here could use a drink, it's you."

"Thanks, Jenna. You're not wrong," she said, taking a long sip of the cocktail. "Oh, wow," she continued with a grimace on her face.

"What is it?"

"I don't know," she said, smacking her lips. "It tastes sort of like poison."

They both shared a laugh.

"Here, let me try it," Jenna said, taking the glass. She took a hefty sip and swished it around in her mouth for a moment. "Oh, that's a negroni. They are a bit of an acquired taste. Here, take mine."

"What's this?"

"It's just a simple Gin and Tonic. You'll enjoy it much more than this one. Trust me."

They sat back and took a few sips of their respective cocktails without speaking. Jenna soon broke the silence.

"So, how long do you think you'll need to stick around here?"

"I don't know. Hopefully not too much longer. If one more person hugs me or tells me how sorry they are for my loss, I might punch them in the mouth. I swear."

"I get that," Jenna said through light laughter. "Your mom seems to be holding up OK. She's talking and laughing with friends. That's a good sign, right?"

"Yeah, I guess," Valerie mumbled as she stirred her drink with the cocktail straw. "I know when we get home it'll be more of the same sadness. I mean, *I get it*, but there's this thick layer of darkness hanging just above each of us at that house right now. I just. I can't take it anymore, you know?"

"Yep. Totally get it."

"She's really trying her best to be there for each of us. I just wish there was something I could do to take some of her pain and burden away."

"You need to think about yourself, too. You know that right?"

"Yeah, yeah. Of course. But you know, it's my mom. Luckily her sister is staying with us for a few more days. So that helps."

"So, she *won't* be alone tonight?"

"No, why?"

"Well," A sly smile washed across Jenna's face. "There just so happens to be a party tonight. And I was wondering—"

"No, nope. Out of the question, Jenna," Valerie cut her off.

"Come on! You *just* agreed that you need to be looking out for yourself too, right? And, you just said you couldn't take another minute of that sad shit at your house. Come on!" Jenna begged.

"It's my fucking *mom*, Jenna. I can't just bail on her."

"You're not bailing! It's not like you're leaving town. Just tell her, you know, it'll help you get your head straight. Say you need a taste of normalcy for one fucking night. It could do you some good."

"You think so?"

"I *know* so. Come on. You *are* coming."

"Alright, I'll talk to her. But I'm not promising anything."

"Oh, stop it. Everything will be fine. *She* will be fine. And you need a little fun in your life again."

"I could use a minor escape, that's true."

"See, your attitude has already changed for the better. You're already looking at the positives. And, consider this. I have some cash, so drinks tonight are on me. We can stop by Richter's Liquor. That creepy 5th year senior is working there tonight, and I can buy you whatever you want to drink."

"Why does that guy serve underaged kids all the time?"

"It's mainly girls. *And* dudes, if those dudes provide invites to parties where there will *be* girls. I don't know. He had a crush on Lexi or something, so he sells to anyone that knows her. Luckily for you, I do know her. Since she's dating my idiotic brother and all."

"Alright. Fuck it. Why not? Let's do it."

"That's the spirit! Now finish your drink. I'm going to hit the bar and steal a couple more rounds for us."

CHAPTER 19

Richter's Liquor was a small and sketchy liquor store that sat on the corner of Hyde Street. Known for its cheap prices on high octane bottles and cans, it was a favorite for folks looking to get tossed without breaking the bank. It also had a reputation for serving underaged high school kids, when the right - or wrong - person was running the counter. A red and yellow overhang with the words "Richter's Liquor" printed graced the small storefront and shooting out towards the street was a neon sign with the word "LIQUOR" beaming in dull yellow. The windows were covered in signs advertising the cheapest 12-packs in town as well as various neon beer and booze signs and posters.

Valerie and Jenna rolled up to the shop in a Gray Prius Uber. The inside of the car smelled of days old incense and stale food. Probably from delivering to hungry locals via the many food delivery services that operated within the city. Techno music blared through the speakers, as though the driver was in a world all his own. He drove down Hyde Street and turned right onto Union, parking against the curb, directly in front of the liquor store.

"You two need me to wait for you or anything?" The driver asked.

"If you don't mind," Jenna said. "We'll only be a minute or two."

"Not a problem. Take your time."

The girls exited the car through the passenger side back door and made their way into Richter's. Inside was decorated and set up like your typical sketchy, neighborhood liquor store. Racks and racks of candy and snacks in the front, followed by even more racks of cheap wine and stacks of warming beer. All the spirits were housed safely behind the counter, along with cigarettes, chewing tobacco and a wide variety of colorful plastic tubes filled with nicotine vape juice.

They entered through the heavy glass door lined with chipped metal, as a bell on a string bounced off the glass, sending dull chimes throughout the air. Standing at the register was an older man who looked lost as he prepared to have his items rang up by the clerk.

"Come on," Jenna instructed. "He won't sell to me if anyone else is in the store. We need to wait for that old dude to beat it."

They immediately turned right down the first aisle, passed the red cooler filled with ice cream bars as they headed straight towards the back of the store. At the back, they stood in front of one of six glass doors that opened to the refrigerated alcohol, beer and various malt liquors.

"So, like I told you. I'm buying so pick out whatever you'd like. Anything that might make you happy. What are you thinking, huh? What would you like to wet that whistle of yours?"

Valerie thought for a moment, admiring all the cheap, warm and close to expiring options that rotted away on the shelves.

"I think I want a 6-pack of Anchor Steam. It was my dad's favorite beer. You know, all the history with San Francisco and all. All the guys down at the shore drank Anchor Steam together. I think that would be a fitting tribute, don't you?"

"One 6-pack of Anchor Steam, coming up!" Jenna said out loud, opening a cooler to retrieve the cardboard box of beer bottles. "OK, what else should we get?"

"How about some vodka and cranberry juice? Those are always refreshing."

"I like the way you think! I can drink those literally all night long. You grab the cranberry juice and meet me in the front."

Jenna made her way to the front of the shop as Valerie turned to her right to pick up a jug of juice. As Jenna reached the counter, she realized the old man was still standing there, looking as lost as ever. Now she didn't care. She wanted to go. No need to stand around in this scummy store any longer than needed. Besides, if she waited much longer, and some cops happened to walk in for a pack of double mint, she didn't want to be around when it happened.

"Come on, man," The clerk said with a roll of the eyes. "Decide already. I've got other customers to serve."

The clerk was Trevor. Older than Jenna and Valerie, but had only recently left the same high school. He had been held back a couple of years and now was attempting to get his GED through night school. He was wearing a yellow plaid flannel and blue jeans and had a mop of blonde hair that flipped all over the top of his head in every which way. Trevor resembled every stoner from a 1980s teen movie and had the attitude to match.

"Uh," The man muttered out. "Let me get, uh, some Marlboro Reds and a bottle of the, uh, Black Velvet."

"Marlboro Reds and Black Velvet. OK. Same fucking color palette as every other drunk evening for you. That wasn't too hard now was it? That'll be $18."

The confused man dropped a crumbled $20 on the counter, then turned to look at Jenna.

"You know, little girl. That stuff'll do more harm than good," The old man said in a shaky voice that dripped in drunkenness.

"Yeah, so will bad attitudes. So why don't you leave me alone, weirdo."

Trevor handed the man a black bag with his cigarettes and whiskey and sent him on his way. He finally motioned for Jenna to approach the counter.

"Well, well, well. If it isn't good ol' Jenna Miller. How have you been, hun?"

"I'm fine, Trevor. Thanks. How are things with you? Still in night school?"

"Sure am," He said, slamming his fingers into the register to calculate the prices. "It's all good. Y'all will see one day. I'll be running this town. One way or another."

"A life of crime? Or fighting those in crime?"

"I haven't decided yet."

They both shared a laugh. Just then, Valerie approached with a jug of cranberry juice.

"Oh, Trevor. This is my friend Valerie. We're getting her fucked up tonight."

"Oh yeah? Any special occasion?"

"Not really," Valerie said with a roll of the eyes as she pushed a long strand of black hair behind her right ear. "My dad just passed away."

"Oh shit. That sucks, man. Well, if anyone deserves a drink or two, it's you, babe."

"Thanks, Trevor," she said. But all she could think to herself was, "*At least he didn't say he was sorry for my loss.*"

"Shit! Almost forgot. I need a bottle of Grey Goose vodka and one of those cotton candy Vector brand Vape pens, please."

"You got it, kid," Trevor said, retrieving both the vodka and the colorful vape pen. "So, where's the party tonight?"

"Sorry Trevor, invite only. It's not my party, so I can't spill the tea."

"Come on, man! You know I'm always cool."

"Hey, I know it. Val here sure knows it. But it isn't our tea to spill, babe. I'll have Brad text you."

"Alright, I guess that's cool. But I better see you both later."

"I am certain that you will."

Jenna swiped a credit card and snatched up two black bags filled with provisions. They said their goodbyes to Trevor and made their way back out to the Uber driver who had waited for them.

"Can you take us to 3646 Leavenworth Street, please?" Jenna asked as they both returned to the back seat.

CHAPTER 20

The Uber slowed to a stop in front of 3646 Leavenworth, and the house was magnificent. A 3-story cream colored, square shaped home with fresh and beautiful white trim around all of its windows and doors. The top level didn't even have windows, it had two sets of French doors, each that opened to their own respective balconies overlooking the street below and the city which surrounded it.

"Is this the place?" The driver asked.

"Sure is. Right up front, or wherever you can get in is fine. We can walk a bit."

They exited again through the back passenger door, wished their driver a good evening, and jumped onto the sidewalk.

"Wow, who's house is this?" Valerie asked, staring up at the gorgeous architecture before her.

"One of Lexi's friends, Brianne. She's cool. I think you met her one time. She came with Lexi to see Brad in one of his track meets."

"That tall, beautiful girl with blonde hair? Sort of looks like a real-life Barbie doll?"

"That's the one. Although, isn't that basically *every* one of Lexi's friends?"

"Hey, you said it, not me." Valerie said with a shy giggle.

From the sidewalk they could hear drum and bass music blaring from inside the home. It was so loud, Valerie was surprised the windows weren't shaking, let alone breaking from the noise. They passed a couple of boys around their age who were out front smoking cigarettes on their way to the front door. Once Jenna pushed the front door open a blast of music that boomed so loud met them. So loud, they could both feel beating inside their chests. The air was dense from sweat, breath and smoke as someone, somewhere, was enjoying some fine, hand rolled joints in the home.

The entrance of the home was littered with people from school and strangers they had never seen or met. The house was kept eerily dark, as the only lights that illuminated the interior were from strategically placed DJ balls that spun, shooting vibrant rays of purples, pinks, blues and greens all over the walls. To the left was the main living room. It appeared that a high-end interior designer decorated it, as everything was a perfect match. From the furniture, to the trinkets to the paint job. Everything was curated perfectly. Valerie immediately felt for the family. Seeing a house this gorgeous being treated as a den of iniquity, she figured would disappoint the parents. Something she had fought hard her entire life to avoid with her own parents. To the right was a staircase that led to the second and third floors. A bright white banister led the way up the hardwood steps. On each step stood multiple teenagers drinking alcoholic beverages from red Solo cups and passing joints around like trading cards.

Past the living room was a giant kitchen decked out in stainless steel appliances, each one Valerie imagined cost more than her own mother's car. In the middle of the elegantly tiled floor was a massive island with brilliant marble countertops. Built into the island was a 4-top stove, and hanging above was a stainless-steel hood and vent. To the left of the kitchen, past the fridge and pantry was a hallway that led to another corridor of the house. To the right of the kitchen was a sort of family room with a nice couch situated in the middle facing a wooden entertainment center equipped with the biggest flat screen TV Valerie had ever seen. These people were doing fine for themselves. Any bad feelings Valerie had escaped her mind knowing, if anything happened in this home or if something broke, they could handle it. Besides, it wasn't her problem.

Her only problem was that Jenna still held onto her Anchor Steam Beer, and she needed one. Badly.

"Hey," Valerie shouted from behind Jenna. "Give me a beer!"

"What? I can't hear you. It's too loud in here."

"I said, give me a beer!"

Jenna nodded and removed two bottles of cold Anchor Steam. She handed one to Valerie and held the other for herself. She popped the tops off and held hers out to perform a proper toast.

"To your Dad. May his memory live on in all the hearts of those who knew and loved him."

"To my Dad!"

They both dipped their heads backwards and placed the bottle to their lips. They began chugging down the cold suds, each one taking an entire bottle down at once. When finished, they each let out a hoot and a holler as, to them, the celebration had begun. Jenna then pulled out two more bottles, popped the tops, and handed one to Valerie.

"Thank you for this, Jenna. I didn't even know how bad I needed a night away."

"What are friends for? I always know what's best for you."

"Hey, I see Spencer! We should go say hi," Valerie shouted.

"No, no. I don't think so."

"Are you *still* shy around him? Come on. He's a fucking dork and you're hot."

"Don't you talk about my future husband like that!" Jenna shouted with a joke smile.

"Future *ex*-husband, maybe."

"That's more like it."

Just then, cutting through the massive crowd of partiers came Brad and Spencer. They raced towards Valerie and Jenna as though they had tractor beams coming from their eyes. Each of them had on a pair of board shorts and a tank top. Brad was wearing a pair of bright pink sunglasses and Spencer wore an inflatable swim toy around his waist that looked like a unicorn.

"Hey ladies!" Spencer shouted, both of his arms held high into the air. In his right hand, he held a red Solo cup.

"What's up Spice Girls?" Brad yelled before chugging down all the contents of whatever drink was in his own cup. "I need another fucking *drink*!"

"Does this house have a pool or something?" Valerie asked.

"No," Spencer replied with a confused look on his face. "Why do you ask?"

"No reason," Valerie said with a shy giggle. "Hey, I'm going to find a bathroom real quick. I'll be back."

Valerie turned and walked through the kitchen and made her way down the unknown, dark corridor in search of a restroom.

"Wait, Valerie," Brad shouted as she left, but she didn't hear him over the loudness of the music and the party. "Where is she going?"

"She's looking for a bathroom, dude. Chill out," Jenna said.

"I wanted to give her a hug and tell her I'm sorry for her loss."

"Yeah, probably not the best thing to do right now, Brad," she said, taking a puff from her cotton candy vape pen.

"What the fuck is this? You're *vaping* now?"

"Yeah so what? Are you *Dad* now?"

"No. But those things are bad for you. Haven't you heard of popcorn lung?"

"Popcorn *what*?"

"Popcorn *lung*. It's where those vape pens make your lungs look like popcorn. It's fucking *gross*."

"You have fucking popcorn for brains, dude. Don't worry about me," she said, taking another puff.

. . .

As Valerie exited the restroom at the end of the dark corridor, she bumped into Lexi and the girl who lived in the elegant home, Brianne. Brianne was just as Valerie remembered. Almost uncomfortably tall, slender and her platinum blonde hair was fluffed and puffed like a mint condition Barbie that had never been unboxed. Her perfect 10 body was barely covered with a thin mini skirt and a crop top that resembled a bra more than anything. Both of which were vibrant blue and bedazzled with sequins that shimmered and shined even in the minimal light. Lexi was a bit overdressed, if Brianne was any comparison. She wore a leopard print skirt with a black spaghetti strap style shirt. Her blonde hair had been left to fall down the sides of her face and crash onto each shoulder.

"Oh my god, Valerie! You made it. I am so happy to see you," Lexi shouted into her ear before embracing her with a full hug. "How are you?"

"I'm, uh. I'm good. Good to see you too, Lexi."

"This is my best friend since, like, forever, Brianne. Her family owns this house. Isn't it gorgeous?"

"Hi Valerie. It is *so* nice to meet you. Thank you for coming," Brianne said in that horrible, nasally voice that seems to just run on and on until the syllables run out of steam and fall off a cliff to their death.

"Hi, yeah. Great to meet you," Valerie said with a touch of condescension. Knowing full and well, they had met before. But it didn't matter. "This is some house. What do your parents do?"

"Um, my dad is only one of the most famous lawyers in all of San Francisco. Hello?"

"Have you ever seen those billboards? Come on, you know the ones! What does it say, Brianne?"

"When you're in trouble, call Samuel Stubble."

"Ah, yes. I've seen those. He's your dad? That's wild," Valerie said with an indiscreet roll of the eyes. She wanted to change the subject. "So, where's Brad?"

"Oh god, don't get me started. Did you see what he's wearing tonight? He's being such an annoying asshole."

"Really? He seemed fine to me."

"Fine? Ugh. I don't think so. If he keeps drinking like this, he's going to be white girl wasted in no time. It's embarrassing."

"Alright, well," Valerie said, ready to escape this conversation at any cost. "Speaking of drinks. I'm fresh out so, I think I'll go grab a refill."

"It was so great to meet you, dear," Brianne said.

"Yeah, thanks."

Valerie reentered the kitchen, promptly poured herself a double vodka and cranberry juice and grabbed a fresh bottle of Anchor Steam beer. She could see Jenna had retreated to the backyard and was exchanging words with Spencer about, god knows what. But it appeared they were having plenty of fun on their own. Valerie noticed the couch in the living room was being ignored, and decided that it could be a perfect place to camp until it was time to go home. She plopped herself down in the dead middle of the couch and downed the entire bottle of beer. Just then, everyone's heads turned towards the kitchen because of a screaming Lexi.

"Brad! Are you fucking kidding me? You are *so* embarrassing!"

Brad had climbed onto the kitchen island with two cans of beer in his hands and was reenacting the move made famous by Stone Cold Steve Austin during his time in wrestling. Standing on the counter, he opened both cans of beer, slammed them together with all his might, sending a healthy splatter of beer and foam all over the kitchen, the partiers below - everything. He then tilted his head, and both beers, and guzzled down whatever suds remained inside the aluminum cans.

"Let's party! Because Stone Cold Brad fucking said so!" He shouted.

"Oh my god. I am *so* leaving," Lexi yelled, both arms in the air as though she was waving an invisible white flag.

Lexi stormed out of the kitchen towards the front door. Once Brad noticed, he jumped down, sprinting after her the moment his feet hit the expensive tile.

"Lexi, come on. Wait, don't go," He pleaded.

"Fuck you, Brad. You've embarrassed me for the last time. I'm out of here," she screamed as she stormed past Valerie, bursting out the front door. She turned and yelled inside, "Call me when you get your head back on straight. Asshole."

The entire party belted out a collective "Ooooooooooooh," at his expense. From the kitchen, a beer can flew by Brad's head. Probably thrown from Brianne, Valerie suspected. But who knew for sure? Brad walked around the couch, his head hanging in shame, and plopped down next to Valerie.

"Well, that didn't go as planned," He said.

"I wouldn't think so. But, hey, I thought it was funny. Lexi doesn't have much of a sense of humor, I guess."

"You know, you're right. She doesn't. Fuck. She's such a buzzkill sometimes, you know?" He asked, sniffling loudly. "Really bums me out."

It was clear, not only from the stunt that had just occurred in the kitchen, but from his stumbling and slurring words, that Brad was deep in his drunkenness. Valerie thought nothing of it, as she was well on her way to the same fate.

"What are we drinking here?" He asked, pointing at her cup.

"Oh, uh. Vodka with cranberry juice. Want a sip?"

"Nah," He shook her off. "I'll get something for myself soon enough." He let out a deep, drunken sigh.

"Are you sure you need any more to drink?"

"Excuse me, judgy," He said, followed by a flirtatious laugh. "I can handle myself. Question is, can you handle yourself?"

"Oh, I can handle myself. Watch your words, mister."

There must have been a drink needed signal flickering somewhere in the house, as Spencer and Jenna entered the room each with a fresh drink in both hands.

"Yeah!" Spencer yelled at the top of his lungs. "Here we go! Let's keep this party going!"

Spencer handed Brad one of the red Solo cups filled with a mystery mixed drink. Jenna did the same to Valerie.

"Say, what do you guys think about moving this party outside?" Jenna asked. "It's way too hot in here. And too *loud*."

"Dude, they have a one-bedroom guest house out back. We can party there. Just the four of us," Spencer instructed.

"I'm down. Valerie? You down?" Brad asked.

"Sure, I'm down. Why not?"

"Let's fucking do it!" Spencer shouted.

Valerie stood with Brad following right behind her. As she walked, she felt something brush her right hand. Looking down, she saw Brad's trembling hand attempting to hold hers. Maybe it was the booze, maybe it was something she had always wanted deep down. She didn't care either way and went with it like it was normal. Like, this was how it should be. And with her hand in his, it felt that way to her. As they maneuvered through the crowd towards the back yard, Spencer picked up a 6-pack of beer and a handle of high-end whiskey that had been left unattended on the counter.

The guest house was decorated identically like the main home, albeit a smaller, miniaturized version. Similar furniture, same layout, same tile. Everything down to the paint was a perfect match of the primary home. Two French doors adorned with elegant curtains opened to the main living room. Tiled flooring stretched the entire small condo and led from the living room to the scaled down kitchen in the back of the structure. To the right of the main entryway was the solitary bedroom and bathroom.

The four friends huddled together in the living room - Valerie and Brad on the couch, while Jenna and Spencer remained on the floor, sitting cross legged - and close. They talked, laughed, talked shit and shared stories of their past and hopes for the future while passing the handle of whiskey around the social circle. Each one, taking down liberal gulp after gulp, filling their blood stream with the intoxicating liquor, allowing their minds to warp into a drunken state of consciousness. As they do when friends reach such a level of intoxication, the conversation soon shifted to a raucous game of Truth or Dare.

"Brad - Truth or Dare," Asked Jenna, speaking through a very noticeable stutter.

"Let's go with dare. I'm feeling frisky tonight."

"Oh, Oh, I got one," Spencer said, changing his position from cross-legged to sitting on the back of his heels. "I dare you to streak through the entire party. Run from the back door and out through the front, fully naked. Straight up birthday suit, bro."

"Get the hell outta here, Spencer," He said, waving his right hand at him. Valerie and Jenna also showed signs of disapproval - namely Jenna, of course.

"That's disgusting, Spencer," Jenna said.

"No way, that would be hilarious. Come on, do it!"

"Absolutely not," Brad said.

"Fine, take a drink."

"Like that's a problem. I've been drinking all night anyway," Brad said with an exaggerated laugh. Valerie and Jenna followed along.

"Fine, whatever. Screw me for trying to spice things up around here."

"Just because you want to see your best friend naked, doesn't mean you need to punish us with that visual," Jenna quipped.

"OK, OK. Jenna, you go."

"Hmm," Jenna muttered, pondering her options. "OH! I've got one. Valerie. Truth or Dare."

"Oh man," she said, her eyes searching the ceiling for the right answer. "I don't know. I guess I'll go truth."

"Ooooh, truth, huh? OK. I was hoping you'd say that. Alright, Valerie. Who was the first guy you were ever with?"

"Billy Donovan. First Grade," she said confidently. "We kissed during recess one day behind the storage container that held all the play equipment. Easy."

"No, no, no," Jenna said, shaking her head with a playful smile. "I mean *with*. Who was the first guy you were *with*."

Valerie's face turned ghostly white. The game was no longer fun for her, and she was no longer interested in participating. She remained silent for a moment, hoping that something - anything - would interrupt and she wouldn't have to answer. If Brad were to run through streaking right now, she would offer to buy him lunch for a year as a thank you.

"Well," She said nervously. "I don't want to play anymore. I'll just drink."

"No, I don't think so," Jenna said. "You've got to answer. Come on, it can't be *that* bad."

"Yeah, not like it's Spencer or something. Wait, is it Spencer?" Brad joked.

"Shut up," Valerie said with a playful punch. "No. Well, truth is. I've never been, you know, *with* a guy."

"No shit?" Jenna asked, her eyes wide open. "You're a virgin?"

Valerie said nothing. She just shrugged in agreement.

"No way! I'm shocked. We're in high school. It's 2021. I thought everyone did it in high school."

"Don't you think I would've told you if I slept with someone already? You're my best friend!"

"I guess that's true," Jenna said, deflated. What she figured would be breaking news for the group turned out to be nothing at all. And being a virgin is nothing to be ashamed of. High school boys are morons, and that's a fact.

"Hold on, wait a minute," Brad said chiming in, sitting forward on the couch. A concerned look washed over his red face. "Are you telling me my little sister has already slept with some guy? You're not a virgin? Tell me that isn't true."

"Well, I mean," Jenna stuttered.

"Who is he?" Brad said with a new-found serious tone. "I want to know who it is right now. I'm going to beat that guy's ass so badly."

"What if it's Spencer," Valerie joked.

"Spencer? Tell me the truth, buddy."

"Ew, no," Jenna said. "Definitely not Spencer."

"What the hell is that? Ew, definitely not Spencer?" Spencer asked, offended.

"Come on, shut up already," Jenna shot back.

"Enough screwing around. Who is he?"

"It's," Jenna paused. "It's no one. I'm a virgin too. I swear. Ugh, fine. See? You got it out of me. And it wasn't even my turn."

"Ok, good," Brad said, relaxing his posture. "Dudes in high school are fucking idiots. Don't waste your time on them. Trust me, I know. I *am* one of them."

"Me too, and he's right," Spencer added.

"Whatever, let's move on," Jenna said. "OK, come on. Someone do me!"

"Yes please," Spencer joked as he lifted the handle of whiskey to his mouth.

"Oh my god, gross. You pig!" Jenna shouted, pushing the bottom of the bottle upwards into his face, causing whiskey to spill down his chin, onto his shirt and the tiled floor.

"You're asking for it now, girly!" Spencer shouted, jumping to his feet.

Jenna burst into uncontrollable laughter, jumped to her feet and sprinted towards the front door of the guest house. Spencer chased her out into the backyard, both of them laughing as they ran. The laughter continued to grow more and more distant as they ran around after one another. Soon, the laughter died, as they had disappeared somewhere into the night together.

"Well, I guess it's just you and me, kid," Brad said, running his palms over his board shorts.

"I guess so," Valerie said. "I haven't drunk this much in, honestly? Maybe never."

"Same here," Brad said. "I mean, I'm always down for a party. But not like this. But, I am having fun. I'm having fun with you."

Valerie smiled to herself as she shifted her view to the floor. Her long black hair fell over her face as she blushed.

"You know, I meant to tell you. I'm so sorry about what happened to your dad. I'm sure that's the last thing you want or need to hear right now. But, I hope you know, if you ever need anything, I'm here for you. Jenna and I both. You mean a lot to us. We love you."

"Thanks, Brad," she said. She considered punching him in the mouth, just like she had promised Jenna she would if anyone said that again. But, from him, it seemed to have meaning behind it. "I love you guys, too. Actually," she began laughing.

"What's so funny?"

"Oh, nothing. Just forget I said anything. I'm drunk."

"So am I. Come on, tell me. What's so funny?"

"Well, the truth is. I've had a crush on you since like, middle school. But, it's fine. It's funny, that's all. I mean, we're older now, and you're with Lexi. It's just, it's funny."

"It's not that funny, really."

"What do you mean?"

"To be honest, I always had a bit of a crush on you, too."

Valerie's eyes lit up like the Rockefeller Center Christmas tree. To say she was shocked would be an understatement.

"You were my sister's friend, and I just felt weird pursuing you. Besides, we we're so young. Then Lexi came along, and, well. I don't even know with her. She's just,"

"She's hot," They said in unison.

"No, that's not *all* there is," Brad chimed in, offended. "She can be a serious pain in my ass. But, she has her moments."

"I guess so."

"Yeah, I guess so, too," Brad said, his face turning a brighter shade of red.

For a moment, if Valerie was correct, she thought she noticed his hands had trembled ever so slightly. She hoped she was right, as hers were trembling, too. She could feel the butterflies stirring within her guts, and wondered if he felt the same.

"I don't know," Brad continued, his tone somber. "She just isn't you. I know that's so weird to hear. Shit, it's even hard to say. But I sort of always figured - no - I always knew. It was supposed to be you."

He turned to Valerie, reached with his right hand and tucked the long strand of hair that hung over her face behind her right ear.

"It was always supposed to be you."

He leaned in ever so slowly, and just as she shut her eyes, she felt his lips land upon hers. One kiss turned to another, more passionate one. She pushed her body close to his, and he followed her lead. His right hand cupped over her right cheek, as she ran her hand up his chest, cupping it over his cheek. They continued to kiss each other as though the world around them was ending. Embracing a moment that if played correctly, could stand the test of time. And at that moment, that is what Valerie hoped. As she ran her finger tips up his chest, she could feel the butterflies within his guts, and they were in a full-fledged war with one another. After what seemed like a short time, they were locked in on one another, and time no longer mattered. Brad pulled back and stared into her eyes. His hand remained on her cheek, and as she pulled away, their eyes locked, and they both smiled.

"I always knew it was supposed to be you," He said in a whisper.

"Me too," she whispered back sweetly.

"I hope I'm not being too up front, but do you want to go into the bedroom? I promise, I'm not looking to take advantage of you. And I know what you said, about being a virgin and all. Truth is, so am I. So, I promise, I'm not trying to just score."

"It's OK. I trust you. And yes, I would like that."

Brad grabbed her by the hand, stood up and helped her off the couch to her feet. She stumbled a bit, and he helped her gain composure. Hand in hand, Brad escorted Valerie into the bedroom. A king-sized bed had been placed in the middle of one wall, with large bed posts that shot straight up into the air. It was adorned with way too many pillows for any bed, each one more elegant than the next. A matching comforter was stretched over, and the walls had bad art hung up in all the wrong places. Brad grabbed the top of the puffy comforter and tossed it towards the end of the bed. He then ran his arm across the head of the bed, removing all the unnecessary pillows, leaving only one for each of them.

"After you," Brad said, waving his right hand over the bed.

Valerie giggled before climbing in, and he soon followed. They held each other for what seemed like hours, kissing, giggling, flirting and everything in between. As the darkness of the sky transformed to a brilliant dark blue, they knew they had outlasted the night. Brad turned over to his back and Valerie rested her head upon his chest, with her right hand under her head, and her left palm open, resting on his chest. His left arm was wrapped around her body, holding her close to him as they drifted to sleep together. Valerie could feel a permanent smile which had taken over her face. She fell asleep happier than she had felt in as long as she could remember.

. . .

Hours later, Valerie woke up from the overwhelming feeling of being shaken. As she opened her eyes, she could feel a chilly hand on her shoulder which produced the obnoxious shaking. She muttered and mumbled to herself as her eyes focused on the unwelcomed light from outside.

"Come on, Brad," she whispered. "We don't have to get up, right? This is just so nice."

"Brad?" A voice said. "What the hell are you talking about?"

Valerie's eyes burst open, and as she raised herself up on the bed, she noticed Brad was gone. One of the many elegant pillows that had been tossed onto the floor had replaced his body, which she cuddled so tightly while she slept.

"What the fuck," She said, rubbing her eyes. When they finally adjusted to the brightness of morning, she saw the hand and shaking was from Jenna.

"Why did you say something about Brad? What the hell happened here last night? Dude, did you sleep with Brad? Fucking gross!"

"Oh my god," she whispered, both hands cupped over her mouth. "No, I did not sleep with your brother."

"Then what the hell happened here? Why did you say his name? Why are you asking for him?"

"Look, OK," Valerie said, rolling her eyes and slamming her hands into the mattress. "We got pretty drunk. We opened up to each other about a lot of things, and we made out. OK? But that's it. We made out, and we fell asleep with each other. But nothing else happened."

"Holy shit," Jenna said, placing her hands over her mouth in shock.

"Where is he anyway?"

"Lexi picked him up like, 20 minutes ago. He ran out of the house like a bat out of hell."

"You've got to be kidding me."

"Yeah, I know."

"You can never say anything about this. You promise me right now. OK? Lexi will kill me."

"Lexi will kill all three of us if she ever finds out. Trust me. Your secret is safe with me. But I am going to punch Brad's fucking lights out for this."

"No, don't," she pleaded. "I'm just as guilty as he is."

"Still, fuck him for leaving you like this. What a dick."

"Yeah. Not my best moment, that's for sure," she said with a roll of the eyes. "Say, what happened to you last night? Huh? Where's Spencer?"

"Don't ask," Jenna said with an exaggerated eye roll. "Do not even ask."

CHAPTER 21

Present...

Brad paced the room holding the wooden baseball bat in front of his body as he moved. He didn't speak out loud, though it was clear, he was in a deep conversation with himself. There was a war within his mind that only he could fight. He needed a plan, and he needed it to work. One that wouldn't fail. He couldn't allow himself to fail. He softly tapped the wooden barrel into his forehead, like he was attempting to dislodge the perfect plan of attack that he hoped was hiding deep within his thoughts.

Valerie found a corner where she could sit and do some thinking of her own. She sat with her legs pulled into her body, her knees pointed at the deteriorated ceiling above them. Her elbows pressed into the tops of her thighs, her hands cupped together where she rested her head. From her hands, a long strand of beads cascaded towards the dusty floor. Under her breath, she continued to whisper to herself. Quiet enough that they weren't discernible to Brad, but just loud enough for her to know she was still alive.

She thought about her mom at home who she had lied to so she could come on this trip. She thought about her siblings who she'd helped raise and instill good values and decisions. And she thought about her father. How he was brutally killed on that fishing dock, and how she needed to make it home - Not just for her own life, but for the lives of her family members. The room remained eerily quiet, the only noises penetrating the thick air around them were the minimal whispers from each of their lips, and Brad's athletic sneakers squeaking and whining across the filthy concrete floor.

"I think I've got it," Brad said with little conviction in his voice, breaking the silence. "Why can't I just go out there and smash him over the head with my new bat?"

Valerie sat in silence without looking up at him. She was mid whisper to herself, and didn't allow Brad's words to break her concentration.

"Valerie," He said again. "What do you think of that plan?"

"What, Brad?" She asked, looking up at him.

"What if I rush out there, you know, like a bat out of hell," He said, swinging the bat around his body. "And I just bash him over the head with this thing a couple of times. That would work, wouldn't it?"

"I think we need a more sophisticated plan."

"But why? He'll never see it coming," He swung the bat around his body again.

"Whoever this guy is," Valerie said, planting her palms on the floor, rising to her feet. "He keeps catching us by surprise. I feel like we need to take the same approach."

Brad dropped the bat to his side, allowing the barrel to smack onto the concrete.

"OK, then. What plan have *you* got?"

"What if we hit him with some sort of diversion?"

"A diversion, huh?" He asked, swinging the bat again like he was trying to hit a fastball. "Now *that* could work. OK. How do we do it?"

Valerie began detailing a plan - Albeit on the fly. This wasn't something she had done before, let alone thought about. But, if all went according to plan, they hoped, wished and prayed it just might work. Valerie and Brad would exit the back of the building. Valerie would turn right and head around the front, between the building and the parking lot where the car sat. Brad would turn left and head around the back of the garage. If - And they knew it was a big if - This masked maniac was still loitering around just outside, waiting for them to emerge, Val would cause a commission to get his attention. She wouldn't need to run or move too fast, as, even with the limited knowledge they had of this psycho, it was clear he didn't move quickly. She would distract him long enough for Brad to sneak up behind him and hit him with the bat. Rendering him unconscious. Then, they could find Jenna, Spencer and Lexi, find their phones and call for help. And if that didn't work—

"Then you run up and bash his mother fucking *brains* in," Valerie added. "You got it?"

"I got it," He assured, holding the bat out in front of his body like Babe Ruth ready to call his home run shot. "You stay back, OK? I don't want him to get his hands on you. And I don't want to splatter you with blood when the bashing begins." He clenched his teeth and dropped the bat from his head downward, mimicking like he was bashing in a skull.

"So, are we ready? Are you sure you want to try this?"

"Don't worry," He said, putting his right hand on her shoulder and looking deep into her eyes. "I've got this. *We've* got this. He can't break us. *We're* going to win."

They're eyes remained locked for what felt like an eternity. In his eyes, Valerie felt a warmth, a softness and a love she hadn't felt in a long time. A warmth, a calm and it felt like love. Just then, she knew the place in his heart she thought he had reserved for her was still vacant. He stared into her eyes as a crooked smile appeared on his face. Valerie blinked her eyes as a comforting smile appeared on hers. With his right hand still on her shoulder, he softly shook her.

"Come on," He whispered. "We've got some business to attend to."

She nodded, returned another smile, and they both walked to the back of the building.

"Brad," she said with a nervous tone, clearing her throat as she spoke. "Be careful, OK?"

"I will," He assured her. "But if I can at least save a couple of us. I'll have done my job."

"What is that supposed to mean?"

"You and I both know, hell, everyone who knows me is well aware of who I am. What kind of guy I am. I haven't been the nicest or the best guy the short time I've been alive. I've done some questionable things at best. The rest, well, I was downright stupid."

He looked at the floor while the thoughts and words inside his skull rattled around like a bingo ball being spun out of control. "Not like it matters if that maniac gets me or not, really."

"Don't you dare say anything like that," she said, a stern warning escaping her throat.

"It's true," He said, his eyes still glued to the floor. "My parents hate me. I mean, my dad. Shit. He's never liked me. I think sometimes he would be happy if I was just out of the picture. And out here, in the desert? He wouldn't even have to deal with it, you know?"

"Hey, fuck your dad," she said, resting her right palm in the middle of his back.

She could feel his heart racing. He was in a panic, but she couldn't blame him. Her heart was raging like a fire out of control, too. Like a tiger in a cage that had been set ablaze with no escape plan. She was terrified, but even worse, Brad was crumbling.

"You stay alive for Jenna, for Spencer, for Lexi. And for *me*. You got that?"

He nodded before looking at her again. This time, it was Brad who felt the loving warmth within her eyes. Something he hadn't realized he needed. Something he hadn't realized he had missed from Val. She almost thought she felt his heart slow to a more manageable pace.

"Can I ask you a question?"

"Sure," she said.

"Before, when you were sitting on the ground. What were you saying to yourself?"

She looked down for a moment. She wasn't ashamed, nor embarrassed. And earlier in the day, she wouldn't have considered sharing any personal details with Brad. But now, things felt different.

"I was," she stuttered. "I was praying."

"Praying? You aren't religious. Are you?"

"Well, no," she said, brushing a few loose strands of hair behind her left ear. "Before my dad died, he gave me this."

Valerie reached into her hoodie pocket, pulling out a small wooden cross connected to a string of beads. "Anytime I feel scared, I hold this cross and I say a prayer. I don't know, it helps me to calm down and to not feel so, well, so alone."

"That's awesome," He said. "I'm sorry about what happened to your dad. I should've been there for you. I should've been a better guy. A better friend."

"Don't. Don't do that," she said with a smile. "You'll always be there now."

They shared a smile before Brad began lifting and moving the steel shelf from the hole in the wall. He wrestled it for a moment, and finally, it gave. The steel legs screeched across the dusty concrete as he gritted his teeth, huffing and puffing with all his might, to reveal the exit.

"Wait, before we go," Valerie said, her cupped hands in front of her body. "Take this. I think you might need it."

She opened her right hand, revealing the cross and strung beads. She extended her hand towards Brad and nodded her head.

"I can't take those," He said.

"Please. Take it. You need all the protection you can get."

"Are you sure?"

"Of course," she said with a smile. "We can't leave anything to chance."

He grabbed the cross and beads, held it and admired it for a moment. He then placed it in his front pocket, as the beads remained outside in view, hanging down against his thigh.

"Thank you, Valerie."

"Give him hell, Brad."

Brad hoisted his body up, sat on the base of the opening in the wall before swinging his legs around and out into the cooling, desert air. He dropped down, his feet landing hard on the sand below. He then reached in to assist Valerie with her exit. When her feet hit the ground, they both found themselves knelt down in the shadows that were produced from the crumbling wall of the abandoned garage.

"Valerie, I truly am sorry for everything," He said, staring at the ground.

Valerie was breathing rapidly. Her chest bounced in and out with every breath as her nerves took hold of her. Brad reached and placed his right hand underneath her chin. He lifted her head so their eyes met.

"It was always supposed to be you. It was always you," He said with a nod. "I am *so* sorry. But I know now, without a doubt in my heart. It was always supposed to be you."

"I know," she said with a confident smile. "Thanks, Brad. Now let's go kill this mother fucker."

CHAPTER 22

As the sun retired for the day beyond the horizon, Mr. Miller walked out through a wide, sliding glass door to a patio deck in the backyard of his large estate. It was quiet where the rich and privileged lived. No sound of rushing traffic or freeways, no gunshots or crime to be seen or heard. Plenty of room and space to distance themselves from those they deemed less respectable and less deserving. He still wore his loose fitting, thin, cloth white pants which were now accompanied by an oversized poncho. Made of thick, colorful threads that resembled a Mexican sarape. Bright blues and yellows paired with strands of black and white. He held two glasses of white wine as he walked across the wooden deck.

The backyard stretched far, and the deck was positioned high above the formal yard, where one could enjoy a cocktail and watch over everyone down below. The yard graced by a beautiful salt water pool with a shimmering black bottom. Within the black were just the tiniest specks of gold that made the water appear to shimmer and shine even more. Perfectly manicured green grass surrounded the pool, just outside of a small concrete lip. Overhead, twinkling string lights stretched from the house to the fence, covering the space above with the perfect ambiance of light.

Laying out on a deck chair was Mrs. Miller. She wore a stark white two-piece bikini, showing off all of her chiseled abs, thighs and the rest of her body that appeared almost photoshopped. Over everything was a sheer white wrap, and her hair pulled back into a very tight ponytail, tied with gold ribbon. All dressed up and nowhere to go. Mr. Miller handed her a glass of chilled white wine and took a seat next to her.

"Here you go, dear," He said.

"Why thank you, my love," she said, taking a generous sip of the chilled liquid. "Any word from the police about the kids?"

"I just got off the phone. That's what took me so long inside. He said he's on his way over now to fill us in on some additional details. I think they traced the kids' phones."

"Well, isn't that convenient," she said, taking in another large sip.

"Convenient how?"

"We just sat down with wine and the cops showed up to ruin it all. I should've expected it."

"Would you stop it? He won't be here long, *that* I can assure you."

"I'm only playing. I'm sure the kids and your precious car are both fine. They're probably living it up in Vegas for the weekend. I think it's great. They're out living life. That's what kids are *supposed* to do at this age."

"So, in your opinion, kids are supposed to commit grand theft auto when they're teenagers? Got it. Noted."

"Thomas, you're being insufferable," she said as she stood from the deck chair. She began walking inside, as she had enough of her husband's poor attitude. When she got inside, she turned back to look at him. "It's only a fucking car. Besides, if something happens, we can afford a new one."

Just then, they heard a chime ring throughout the home.

"Well, just in time," she said with a sarcastic tone.

"Just in time for what?"

"Well, I'm leaving you outside to deal with your horrible, pathetic attitude towards parenting. Now you won't be alone. The cop can keep you company."

"Would you stop?" He shouted. "I'm not being a negligent parent. Actions have consequences, you know that. Brad needs to learn a lesson. I'm not really going to have him thrown in jail. Just, calm down."

"Oh, I *am* calm. Hey, if the cop is going to enjoy wine with you tonight, you know, because *I won't* be. Maybe he can sleep with you tonight, too. Because guess what," she leaned out the door and dropped her voice to a whisper. "I won't be doing *that* either."

Mr. Miller lifted his glass back all the way, filling his mouth with the cold wine. With one big swallow, he polished off the entire glass. His eyes watered as he grimaced from the slight burn. Then, with his right wrist, he wiped the excess from his lips. It wasn't long before Officer Pullman made his way out onto the deck to join him.

"Good Evening, Mr. Miller. Do you mind if I have a seat?"

"Be my guest," He replied, motioning to the deck chair Mrs. Miller had left warm for him.

"Nice place you've got here. You must be the envy of all your friends."

"Something like that," He said without making eye contact. "What have you got for me?"

"Well," Officer Pullman said, opening a manila folder on his lap. He pulled out a few single slips of white paper and began shuffling through them. "We haven't found your kids yet. Or your car. But, we traced your son and daughter's cell phones."

Pullman handed him the sheets of paper, each detailing the finding for their respective cell phones.

"As you can see from these maps, the last cell tower either of their phones pinged was in a small desert town called Baker."

"Baker? Is that close to Vegas?"

"Sort of. It's on the way to Vegas. It sits right off the 15 freeway. About 90 minutes outside of Las Vegas, though."

"So they're in Baker, then? Did you call the Baker police, or whoever patrols that town to pick them up?"

"We have in fact contacted the highway patrol to be on the lookout. But unfortunately, no, we haven't found them yet."

"So, you think they're still in Baker?"

"That would be my hope, yes."

"OK then," Mr. Miller said as he stood up. "Thank you for coming by. I'll show you out."

"Uh, before I go, Mr. Miller," Pullman said, a very serious tone seasoning his words. "I wondered if I could give you some unsolicited advice."

"Yeah, uh, sure," He replied, scratching the back of his head, confused.

"So, as a parent myself, I know I don't want anyone telling me how to raise or handle my kids. I've got 3 at home. Much younger than yours, but still—"

"OK, come on," Mr. Miller said, his patience wearing thin. "Out with it."

"I just think that you should try to have a bit more compassion for your children, sir. You seem overly worried about a car, much less so about the 5 lives who were riding within it."

Mr. Miller let out a sharp giggle, followed by a deep sigh. He planted his hands on his hips and shook his head.

"A car, no matter how expensive, can be replaced, Mr. Miller. Children can't be. But, I think deep down you know this."

"Hey, how about you mind your own business here?"

"Protecting the safety of the public *is* my business, Mr. Miller. And that includes your children, as well as the three other kids with them."

"Why don't you leave the parenting of my children to me and you can go save a cat from a tree or something."

"With all due respect, I'm afraid you've got your bullshit stereotypes mixed up."

Officer Pullman walked past Mr. Miller and entered back into the home, as he had enough and was ready to leave. He had enough of Mr. Miller's attitude towards parenting, his job and life in general. As he walked, Mr. Miller stared at him with an obvious level of confusion in his eyes. Once he was inside, he turned back.

"Firefighters rescue cats from trees. Cops, like me. Well, we just sit around drinking coffee and eating donuts all day. Remember?" He said with a sly smile. "Good day, sir."

After Officer Pullman excused himself from the home, Mr. Miller flew in the back door like a tornado out of control.

"Babe," He screamed up the stairs. "Get out here, now!"

Mrs. Miller emerged from the hallway and peered down the stairs at her jerk of a husband. It was written all over her face - She had enough of him, too.

"What is it? Why the hell are you screaming at me?"

"Pack a light bag and get some sleep," He said as he removed a duffel bag from a downstairs closet. "Bright and early, we're headed to Baker, California."

CHAPTER 23

Brad crept as silently as his large, athletic body would allow towards the back corner of the old garage. He wrapped his fingertips around the edge of the wall while pulling his knelt body forward to peer around. The back of the building was covered in shadows, even at night, creating an eerie darkness. Even the minimal light of the moon was blocked, almost like evil itself was present. This let Brad know one thing for sure - The man was close by.

"I don't see him," He whispered over his right shoulder.

Valerie nodded, lifted her right hand and with her index and middle finger pointed at her eyes, then at the opposite edge of the building. Speaking only in motions now, Brad nodded in agreement.

She crept, close to the ground so that she could look around the front of the building.

"Bingo," she whispered.

Brad shot around as Valerie put her right hand in the air to stop him and any movement he might make.

"He's by the parking lot," she whispered over her shoulder.

Staying low to the ground, she hurried back to Brad to finalize the final step in the plan. Their ultimate attack for survival.

"OK," she whispered, clunking down hard on the back of her feet. "He's standing by the parking lot at the other side of the building. So, you head around the back, *quietly*. When you reach the edge of the building,

I'll jump out and get his attention. When he looks at me or heads my way, you jump out and bash that piece of shit until his head is a pancake. You got it?"

"Got it," Brad said. "Don't get too close to him, OK? I don't want him to get a piece of you."

"Don't worry about me. I got this. But *do not* hesitate. When you get to him, you take him out. We've got one chance here. Let's make it count."

Brad nodded with a mask of confidence wrapping his face. He extended his right hand and Valerie pressed her's into his. Their hands connected at the thumbs with their fingers crashing over each other.

"Here goes nothing," Valerie said.

"Give 'em hell, kid," Brad replied with a nod.

Still crouched, Valerie maneuvered to the edge of the building. She turned to look back over her shoulder at Brad, but he was already gone. The plan was in motion. There was no turning back. It was now or never.

Valerie closed her eyes, took in a deep breath and held it for a long moment. She opened her eyes as she exhaled and stared out at pure nothingness in the desert. Again, her mother's face flashed through her mind. Followed by her siblings, and then her father. She had to succeed. There was no other way.

In a flash, she jumped to her feet and walked out of the shadows. Standing underneath one of the flickering street lights of the parking lot, she could see the masked maniac. He stood still, motionless, statuesque. If she hadn't known any better, she might have thought he had left a mannequin there. A diversion of his own to trick them out of the building. But she was certain, she was confident. She had to be.

"Hey, you gross mother fucker!" She shouted.

Slowly the masked head turned towards her. Her blood ran cold as she gasped for air. Terror washed over her body from the outside in, as the man turned his body. He took a long, labored step towards her, dragging his bad leg behind him across the pavement. Dangling from his right hand was the rusty meat hook. He had been waiting them out, and here she was. One labored step, followed by another. The surrounding air was silent as death, and Valerie could hear as his worn-out leather boots scraped as they dragged across the asphalt.

From the opposite side of the building, Valerie saw Brad as he took light steps from the shadows into the light. He held the baseball bat handle in his hands, the barrel up high in the air above his head as he crept towards the monster. The plan was working as it was written. They figured Brad was faster and smarter than the attacker, and, of course, he was unaware anyone was behind him. Even from a faraway vantage point, Valerie could see Brad's eyes opened wide. Like a starving, wild animal in the midst of a hunt, ready to devour his kill. He kept his eyes locked on the man so hard that he didn't even notice the debris hiding in the sand at his feet.

Just then, Brad's foot hit an old oil can, sending it sputtering and clanking across the asphalt. He froze, looked down at the can, then back at the man who was just out of reach. The man stopped in his tracks and turned his head to the left at the noise.

"Oh shit," Brad muttered. "Fuck this!"

Brad burst into a full sprint at the man. The plan might have been foiled, but it wasn't dead. Not yet.

"Brad, no!" Valerie shouted, both of her hands outstretched as though she might be able to stop him. But it was too late.

The man spun around as Brad approached. With his right hand, the man swung that rusty meat hook at Brad's torso. Brad didn't see it coming until the hook was already traveling at him. He planted his feet into the ground, pushing backwards with all that he had. The meat hook sliced through his shirt, just missing skin. He took another few steps back, holding the bat in his right hand. With his left, he checked his shirt to see the slice that had been cut through and to check for blood.

"You son of a bitch!" Brad screamed. "I'll fucking *kill* you!"

Brad held the bat by the handle with both hands, positioned his body like he was about to face Nolan Ryan with a batting stance, and swung the bat with every fiber of strength he had within his body. The bat whipped through the air so quick, you could almost hear a swoosh. The swing connected with the man's left side, pummeling his ribs.

He let out a painful and strained groan as he fell back a couple of steps. He leaned down with his left arms pressed hard into his abdomen. As he looked up to Brad, he put both hands in front of his body as Brad charged. He planted his left foot into the ground, lifting his right and delivering a hard kick to the man's chest. Immediately he fell to the ground, landing hard on his back. A loud gasp escaped from the man's throat, as it sounded like he had knocked the wind out of his lungs.

Brad jumped and stood over him, with a foot on either side of his body. Sounds like a rabid dog poured out of his mouth as he seethed. Drool and spit dripped from his mouth, his eyes squinted in fury, and his knuckles white from grasping the handle of the wooden bat.

He tried to swing the bat downward to strike the man, but he fought off each blow. The barrel bounced off his forearms, wrists and hands as he tried to strike him. Brad unlocked his knees and let his body fall, landing on the man's chest. He began pummeling him with punches to the face. One after another, striking the man until he began to go limp. Brad stood up, wiped his mouth with the back of his right hand and lifted the bat high above his head. He was looking to land one, last fatal blow to the head, caving it into a pancake. Just like Valerie had instructed.

"See you in hell, you—"

Brad's words floated through the air like a dead leaf in fall. A sentence that trailed off and never finished.

With the meat hook in his right hand, the maniac jumped to his knees and swung upwards at Brad, connecting the sharp point of the hook directly underneath his jaw. The point stabbed through the soft flesh just under his jaw, cracked through the bone, and protruded out of his mouth. Brad let out a horrific gasp of air as he screamed and shrieked in both pain and terror. He stumbled back a few steps before he regained his composure, dropping the bat as he went. The bat hit the asphalt, pinging and crackling along until it came to a stop far enough away, he could no longer reach it.

The man stood up slowly, breathing heavily and grotesque. Blood had begun to spill out through the mouth holes of the mask that still covered his face, though askew from the pounding he had endured. He straightened it so he could see Brad. Brad felt his face, jaw and mouth and attempted to tear the meat hook from his flesh, but it wouldn't budge. He began swinging at the masked man, missing each and every time. Brad cowered, placing both his open palms on his thighs as he attempted to catch his breath and allow his nerves to catch with his new reality. He lifted his head towards the man as a generous amount of blood poured from his mouth to the ground. He wound up, taking another haymaker swing, but the man pushed it away with his left arm while grabbing the handle of the meat hook with his right hand.

The man held the meat hook and stared deep into Brad's shivering eyes. Brad could see every ounce of evil beaming from his dark eye sockets. Then, the man pushed Brad away from him, grabbed the handle of the hook and as Brad fell backwards, he pulled the hook towards himself. The air filled with slight sounds of bone, muscle and tendons as they tore, snapped and pulled out of place. Brad let out a painful cry - Sharp and high pitched. Brad wobbled a bit, every bit of his body trembling and shaking uncontrollably as it shut down.

He looked to his left as he saw Valerie, just far enough away yet so very close. Their eyes met, as Brad raised his right hand just high enough to catch her attention. Dangling from his hand were the beads she had handed to him before the plan went awry. He lifted his right hand to his chest, pressing the cross and beads into his body and held them tightly against his heart. He shut his eyes for a long moment before opening them again, staring right at Valerie. She knew what that meant. Brad was saying goodbye.

The masked man grabbed the hook again with his right hand and lifted his good leg, pressing it hard into Brad's abdomen. He pushed back with his foot as he pulled once, then again on the hook as it grasped Brad's jaw. This pull, again, filled the air with soft sounds of bone cracking. The second pull tore Brad's jaw clean off his skull. Bone and connective tissues snapped and cracked as his lower jaw became suspended within his mutilated flesh. Like a horse shoe hanging carelessly in a bowl of jello. Brad fell to his knees, settling upright as his body sat on the back of his legs and feet.

The masked man dragged his own body to where the bat had settled. He lifted it and sauntered back to Brad, positioning himself behind him. He looked at Valerie, who stood in shock. She couldn't move. She didn't want to see what was about to happen, yet she was frozen there. Frozen in a nightmare that was never ending.

He lifted the bat high above his head, striking it down onto Brad's head. Brad fell forward, landing flat on his chest. Again and again he struck Brad in the back of the head with the bat, flattening his head and skull into the ground. All the while, he kept his eyes locked onto Valerie.

He let go of the bat and again it clinked and clanked, bouncing off the hard ground as it rolled away. He bent down, tore the meat hook away from Brad's mangled skull and pointed it towards Valerie. Then, took a long, labored step in her direction.

Valerie gasped, turned from him and ran as fast as she could into the darkness of night. Away from her friends and away from the building that had provided a false sense of security. She didn't know where she would go, and at that moment, she didn't care. As long as it was as far away from this masked murderer, it didn't matter. So, she ran, and she ran. Through the desert - Alone, cold and scared.

CHAPTER 24

Valerie ran. Deep into the darkness of night, and the desolation of the California desert, she ran. Leaving behind the crumbling garage and store, the expensive car, the madman and, worst of all, her friends - whatever was left of each of them. She hadn't seen what occurred with Spencer, Jenna or Lexi, and after what she had witnessed with Brad, she was glad that she hadn't. But deep down in a place where the outside light never shines, burns a small flicker of hope that maybe, just maybe, one, if not the rest of them, might still be alive. She figured that masked freak had done something awful to each of them. But if she could just find someone - anyone or anything - she wanted to believe they could be saved. Hope still lived inside of Valerie. And sometimes, hope is all you need.

She ran for what seemed like an eternity. Longer than she had run in as long as she could remember. Possibly, longer than she had ever ran in her entire life. Her arms thrust backwards and forwards, her head straight down, her legs chugging along harder and harder than she had ever attempted to run. She pushed her body to the limit to get away from that sick psychopath. She couldn't even say "human being." No, that was no human being to Valerie. That was a monster. A nightmare come to life, and she needed to get as far away as possible. So, she ran. She ran until her muscles tore and until her lungs gave out. She ran until her feet bled and until her veins pumped with battery acid. There was no way to be certain, but she figured she must have run for miles already. All that distance in pure darkness, alone. No living, breathing being in sight. No street lamps, no 7-11's. No comfort and no safety. Now, at this moment, it was her versus the landscape. And even worse, it had become her versus herself. But she couldn't give in. That little light of hope burning deep within her spirit gave her all the courage she needed to keep going. To keep pushing. To stay alive.

Just then, over the horizon something appeared. The faintest blip of dull yellow light shot into the air. From such a far distance, it appeared like nothing at all. Smaller than a single star in the frozen night sky, but to Valerie, it was everything. That faint, miniscule blip of yellow sparkled and danced in the distance like a beacon calling Valerie home. Like a lighthouse to a sinking ship just off the coast, caught in the storm of its lifetime. The storm within her was no different, nor was this call to safety. The hull of her body was cracking, but it wasn't lost. Not yet.

She pushed on towards what she believed was real. "*Please, don't be a mirage,*" she thought to herself repeatedly. She had never seen a mirage, but had heard of them and how they were always associated with people who found themselves in trouble in the desert. "*Please be real,*" she thought to herself. "*Please, don't be a mirage.*"

As she trudged on, the slight blip of light grew larger and more intense. In fact, it wasn't just one blip. There were many blips. With every pump of her legs an array of lights became clearer. Different shades of dull yellow and bright white. Some steady, some flickering, but each one, a sign of life. And that is all Valerie needed. That hope inside of her had proven true thus far. The closer she got to the lights, the more her eyes could see what they illuminated beneath them. She had run so far into the darkness that she had found a roadside rest stop. She had forgotten that, before they exited to find the charging station for the Zeus, they had passed on this rest stop because it had no charging stations available for use. Now she didn't need a charging station. She needed a sign of life, a phone and if at all possible, a damn drink of water.

Once she saw the rest stop, somehow, she found the strength to increase her speed. Her body had become exhausted and her legs had taken enough, and as she tried to push on, her legs gave out and she crashed into the sand. She fell forward, pushing her palms into the desert floor as she fell. Once her body landed, she tumbled over herself a few times, landing on her left side. She rolled on to her back and gazed up at the starry sky as her lungs burst in and out, trying to fill her blood with enough oxygen to keep going. She could see her hooded sweatshirt lifting and falling rapidly as her heart beat and burst through her chest.

"I'm not going to make it," she thought to herself. *"I can't do this anymore."*

She closed her eyes as she dreamt about her family. How devastated and broken her mother was when her father died. How she comforted her siblings for months when her mother became absent from the sinking feeling of depression and loneliness. How she cuddled her mother at night, brushing her thick, black hair back over her head as she wept, whispering, "Everything will be fine, Momma. I promise." And how she couldn't make her mother go through that pain again. Anyone with an outside perspective would try to explain to Valerie that none of this was her fault. But it wouldn't matter. She blamed herself now, and knew she would in whatever afterlife was to come, as well. The pain in her mind, heart and physical body became too much to bear. As her eyes welled with tears, they began flooding down her cheeks to the sand. She shut her eyes tight as she cried herself sick. She dug her open hands deep into the dirt, clenched her fists, filling her hands with earth and screamed with everything she had left inside of her spirit. Banging her closed fists into the sand, she screamed and screamed. So loud that she thought blood may burst from her throat and pour down her lips.

The sound of a blasting horn that filled the silence awakened her. She thought she had died, and the heavens were opening to accept her. She remained there, on her back, as an eerie sense of calm washed over her body. After a few moments, something else brought her back down to earth.

"Hey!" A man's voice shouted. "Is someone there? Hello? Are you OK out there?"

Valerie's eyes shot wide open as she dug her hands into the sand, wrestling herself up to her knees. Just outside of the rest stop parked along the far side of the parking lot was a semi-truck. She couldn't believe her eyes. *Safety*. It was so close she could almost taste it.

"Is someone there?" The voice yelled again. "Hello? Do you need help?"

She squinted her eyes at the truck when she noticed something that shot excitement through her entire body like a bolt of lightning. The trailer attached to the truck was a SWIFT trailer.

"Swift," she muttered. Her voice grew in intensity as did her excitement. "Swift. Swift! SWIFT! I win, mother fucker! Swift! I fucking win!"

She forced herself to her feet and pushed along with any energy she could muster towards that Swift truck.

"Hey! Help me!" She screamed as she ran, flailing her arms as she went. "Please! Please help me!"

The man burst into a full sprint towards Valerie. Before he could reach her, her legs gave out yet again. As she fell, the man jumped and slid on his knees across the dirt, catching her in his arms and lap as she crashed into him. Valerie began grabbing at his arms, hands, body and face, breathing hard and furious. She needed to know if this was real. If he was real.

"Are you OK?" The man asked in a panicked tone. "What the hell are you doing out here all by yourself?"

"Help me! Please," she shrieked through half breaths. "A man. That man. He's trying to kill me. He, he killed my friends. Please."

"It's OK," He whispered, followed by a low shushing noise. "I've got you, Ma'am. Come on, let's get you to my truck."

He was an older man who appeared at the business end of his 50s. He was tall, rail thin with white hair on the sides of his head and a matching white, scraggly beard over his wrinkled face, wearing dusty old overalls over a red and black plaid long sleeve flannel shirt. A torn trucker hat rested upon his head covering a wasteland of bald skin.

He assisted Valerie to her feet, throwing her right arm over his shoulders as he escorted her across the desert to his truck.

"What happened to you, Ma'am?" He asked sweetly as they walked.

Valerie couldn't speak as she continued to try her best to breathe. She just shook her head over and over again as he helped her walk to safety. When they reached the truck, he reached up to open the passenger side door so she could crawl in.

"Come on, dear," He said, grabbing her left hand and holding on. "It's OK dear. Watch your step. Go ahead. Crawl on up into the cab. You'll be safe now, I promise. I'll get you out of here. Come on, up you go."

She pressed her feet into the steel step while grabbing hold of the safety bar on the side of the truck body. She pulled and strained as she hoisted herself upwards. The man grabbed her by the waist and assisted pushing her into the cabin.

"It's OK, dear," The man whispered. "I'm not getting fresh, I swear. Just trying to help you up and in. It's OK. Go ahead, take a seat."

Once in the cab, she let every muscle crumble at once as she crashed into the seat. Her head fell back against the headrest, as her eyes shut. The man stood on the step so that he was at eye level with Valerie. He continued to make soft and sweet shushing sounds as he reached far behind the seat pulling out an old blanket. He draped it over her body to keep warm and looked down at her as he noticed a sense of comfort had washed over her.

"It's OK, dear," He whispered. "You're safe and sound now."

He jumped off the step and slammed the door shut with Valerie inside the truck. He removed his cap and wiped the sweat from his brow with the sleeve of his flannel shirt letting out a "*Phew*" as he went. He turned to his right to walk around the front of the truck and climb into the driver's seat, but before he made it around the engine compartment, something caught his eye at the far end of the parking lot of the rest stop. A rusty, old blue Jeep was parked in a far-off spot. The once brightly painted white top, looked like years and years of neglect had allowed rust to take over. It looked like it had been stranded in an odd place and time, beaten to death by the elements and the sun for decades.

"Huh," The man said out loud. "I don't remember seeing that Jeep here before."

CHAPTER 25

Valerie sank her body deep into the passenger seat and wrapped the blanket around her shivering body. She was drenched in sweat and had been pelted by the constantly dropping desert temperatures and wind that whipped every inch of her body as she ran those miles to safety. The cooling temperature of her body only made the shaking from absolute fear that had consumed her that much worse. Part of her mind eased, though she knew she couldn't let her guard down just yet. She didn't know this trucker, and in any other instance, she would never allow a stranger to hoist her body into a strange truck in the middle of the night. But when she compared this to the alternative that had presented itself, she would take a soft blanket and a warm truck cabin any day over a meat hook slicing her throat and being left for dead in a lonely parking lot just outside of Baker, California.

The driver side door shot open as the trucker pulled himself up and into the cabin as he rested in the seat next to her. He rubbed his open palms on the pant legs of his overalls and let out one of the deepest sighs Valerie had ever heard.

"My name's Tom," He said, reaching his right hand towards Valerie. "What's your name?"

Valerie paused for a moment and watched his hand, then looked back at his face. He seemed nice enough. But until she was safe in the arms of the police or her mother, she would keep anyone and everyone at an arm's distance.

"Valerie," she said with trembling words. She opened the blanket and softly shook his hand. "You're Tom the Trucker?"

"I know, I know," Tom said with a shy laugh. He took off his hat and ran his right hand over the top of his head. "Trust me, I get plenty of odd comments from all the other road warriors out there. But that's OK. The road is what I love. Let them say whatever they want."

Again, Valerie wrapped the blanket tight around her body. She nodded along with Tom the Trucker as he spoke about his love of being on the road. She imagined for a moment that it must be a peaceful existence. Living life on your own terms. Cruising around the country day in and day out. Seeing such interesting people and places every day. Then again, how often did Tom the Trucker leave a route to see anything magical that the country offered? He was probably more used to rest stops, fast food and weirdos.

"Say," Tom said, turning to reach into the back of the truck cab. "Do you need a drink? I've got this case of water bottles back here. They're nothing too special—"

The second his hand appeared with a fresh water bottle, Valerie swiped it from him like a snake biting its prey. She uncapped the bottle, tilted her head back and guzzled down the lukewarm liquid in record time.

"They're not cold or nothing," He continued. He shook his head lightly. "Boy, you sure we're thirsty. Say, what are you doing out here all by your lonesome, anyway?"

"Can I have another?" She asked, not acknowledging his question.

"Oh yeah. Of course. Have as many as you'd like." He reached into the back to retrieve a couple more fresh bottles. He handed two to her and kept one for himself. "Don't worry about the water. I stock up at Costco before these big trips. Really saves money on a long drive. Keeps me from stopping, too."

She guzzled down the second bottle just as quickly as the first, holding on to the third for later.

"Thank you for helping me," she said.

"What happened to you tonight? You look like a tornado or something hit you."

"Can we get out of here? I'll tell you the entire story. We just need to get the hell out of here *now*. And we need to call the police."

"Whoa, whoa. Call the police? What happened out there?"

"My friends and I stopped a few miles away. Some place called Halloran Summit, I think."

"Halloran Summit?" His eyes shot open. "You ran all the way from Halloran Summit? That's close to 5 miles!"

"There's some, I don't know. A man. He's a fucking monster. He killed one of my friends. I saw him do it. I don't know what happened to the others. They might be dead too. All I know is, we need to get out of here right away. He's going to be looking for me. And if he finds me, he'll kill us both."

"Kill us? Are you sure about all this?"

"Yes! I saw him. He killed my friend. He crushed his skull with a baseball bat right in front of me."

"Who is this man? Why would he do such a thing?"

"I told you, I don't *know* who he is. All I know if we need to get the fuck out of here right *now!*"

"OK, OK. Where should we go?"

"There was a little town back a few miles, right? There has to be police or *someone* there that can help."

"That's Baker," He said with excitement. "We can get you help in Baker. OK. I need to remove the wheel chocks and we can hit the road. As soon as the rubber meets the road, I can call this in on my radio. Maybe the police can meet us in town."

Tom opened the door and hopped out of the truck.

"Don't worry your little head," He said, looking up into the cab. "We'll get you to safety before you know it."

Tom shut the door and made his way to the back of the trailer to remove the encumbrances from each wheel. The chocks were bright yellow and had been shoved deep under two of the back wheels of the trailer. Protruding from each was a long, yellow handle that raised about waist high. This made for easy usage, both in installation and removal before travel. When the driver side door shut, Valerie noticed the massive mirror that sat just outside the window had been positioned so that she could see every movement Tom the Trucker made. She watched as he wrapped his hands around the handle and began wrestling the chock from underneath one of the back wheels. She imagined it must be heavy, as he wrestled with it for a good amount of time before he finally got it to budge. Although, Tom the Trucker wasn't in peak shape. He was skin and bones. So, any activity that required muscle might become a chore for someone like good old Tom.

She watched him, wondering if she should offer to help. After all, if it weren't for Tom, she might still be running in the darkness. Alone, exhausted, fearing for her life. Instead, she wrapped the blanket tighter and set her head back against the vinyl seat. It was cold, but somehow felt great against her damp, sweaty hair. She closed her eyes and took a deep breath. It had been hours since she felt any sense of comfort. Now that she had it, she didn't want to let it go. Especially to fight with a heavy wheel chock.

Her mind had drifted off to another place when she was shot back into reality. A loud crash of steel against steel. She glanced to the driver side mirror to see what Tom the Trucker had done. He must have stored those heavy items within metal storage bins that had were positioned underneath the trailer itself. She saw Tom as he rubbed his hands together.

Just then, Valerie noticed something in the darkness behind Tom. She thought maybe her mind was playing tricks on her, so she leaned over towards the driver seat for a closer look. She squinted her eyes at the mirror and focused in on the mysterious object. Her eyes shot open wide when her brain caught on. Tom the Trucker wasn't alone. The masked maniac had found them both.

"Tom!" She shrieked

He didn't budge. Nor did the figure looming behind him. He stood deathly still, only shifting his head even further to the right, admiring Tom. She pushed her body off the seat and lunged toward the rope that hung above the driver seat. She caught it with her right hand and thrust it downward. A roaring horn burst out and echoed throughout the air. She pulled it again and again to get Tom's attention. She pulled her body up and found herself sitting behind the wheel. She grasped the wheel while leaning towards the mirror.

"Tom! Get out of there! Tom, run!" She screamed.

Tom's body jerked at the sudden blaring horn, as though a burst of electricity had hit him. But it was too late for good old Tom.

The masked man reared back and swung with his right arm, dragging the meat hook upwards along Tom's spine. He let out a horrific shriek of pain as both of his arms shot up into the air and he shot forward. Like the feeling of ice-cold water splashed on your back when you don't expect it. He twisted his body, falling against the trailer with his now sliced open back. Blood stains grew from underneath his overalls as it flooded from the abdomen length gash.

Valerie screamed while covering her mouth with both hands. The masked man heard the screams and turned his head just enough to see her. Their eyes met in the mirror, and she was almost certain she saw him laughing under Spencer's mask.

Again, he pulled his right hand behind his back, swung around his body and cut through Tom's belly. Blood burst from the gaping wound dousing the dirt like a busted sprinkler. He wrapped his arms across his belly as he fell to his knees. When he hit the ground, the rest of his body fell forward with enough force that his forehead crashed into the soil. Through his clasped fingers, blood poured like a fish tank whose glass had shattered and his intestines fell into his open hands, covering his forearms as they hung from his open gut. Using his good foot, the masked man kicked Tom's body, forcing him to land on his right side. There was nothing anyone could have done. Tom was gone. A helpless victim in someone else's disgusting game. The game was now Valerie's. And she needed to win.

Again, she found herself alone. The only help within miles had been sliced wide open right before her eyes. After hitting the lock on the driver door, Valerie dove back to the passenger seat. She grasped the door handle so tight she could have broken it clear off. She looked in the mirror and saw that the coast was clear. If she didn't try to make her move now, she might as well sit and wait to die inside that truck. She pulled the handle, pressed her feet against the inside of the door and pushed with all her strength. With her hands planted into the vinyl seat, she pushed her body up and out of the truck. The drop was farther than expected, and when her feet hit the ground, she stumbled forward, reaching her hands out to break her fall. Her open palms scraped across the pavement of the road and she moved with such momentum, her body twisted and rolled over a couple of times across the pavement.

She jumped to her feet and stared out at the vast emptiness from which she had come. Could she run all the way back to that place? Even if she could, did she want to? "*Hell no*," she thought to herself. She never wanted to face that place again. She wanted to forget every single second she had spent at Halloran Summit Road. Valerie turned as she attempted to run in the opposite direction, but it was no use. Her body connected hard into the massive body of the maniac. She pushed him away from her, but he didn't budge. Instead, the push only knocked her back a step or two.

"What the fuck do you want from us!" Valerie yelled.

She let out a fierce scream as she clenched her fists. She wound up and took a swing at him. He lifted his left hand, blocking the blow and grabbed her by her right forearm. He forced her arm downwards as he raised his right hand high into the air. With a single swipe, the meat hook sliced through Valerie's left cheek, cutting her face into two.

An intense yelp escaped from her throat as she cupped her hands over her face. She couldn't see anything, but could feel the warm trickle of blood as it dripped through her fingers and down her face to her body. She stumbled backwards, tripping over her own feet. When her exhausted body fell, her head connected with the steel step just underneath the open passenger door of the truck, sending her entire world into blackness in an instant.

He left her there, lying unconscious, blood gushing from both her face and the back of her head. Soon, the area was illuminated by dull yellow headlights from the rundown Jeep as it approached. He pulled alongside the truck and jumped out. He flicked open the back hatch, grabbed Valerie from under her arms and brutally hoisted her body up and into the back. He then emerged from the back of the semi-trailer, his hands underneath Tom's body as he pulled and dragged him through the dirt. He lifted his limp and lifeless body into the back of the vehicle, shutting the back hatch before driving into the desert towards Halloran Summit Road.

CHAPTER 26

Valerie slowly came to, as did all of her sleeping senses. She could barely lift her head as her eyelids opened ever so slightly. Everything in her vision was a blur as she blinked repeatedly, hoping to focus in on something - anything - to let her know where she was, and to let her know if she was alive or dead. Her chin had been buried deep into her chest, and as she lifted the pain in her neck and shoulders burned like a 4-alarm fire. The ache and pain in her joints was deep, and the pain was almost too much to handle. As her head lifted from her chest, drool and spit poured out of the corner of her mouth to her raggedy, blood soaked hooded sweatshirt. She tried to lift her right hand to rub the muck from her eyes, but her arm wouldn't budge. She shook her head in a fury, blinking and rolling her eyes side to side as her new world came into focus.

She looked down at her hands, noticing that she had been strapped to a rolling desk chair. Her wrists were bound to the arms of the chair by chains that had been wrapped multiple times from her fingers to her forearms. She tried pulling her arms upwards, but the chains didn't allow for any movement. She wriggled her fingertips and stretched them outwards to allow some blood to flow. The awful feeling of pins and needles had taken over her fingers, hands and arms, as those chains had cut off the ability to feel anything at all.

She tried to kick her feet, but they also wouldn't budge. She leaned forward as far as her body would allow to see that her ankles were also chained. Those chains had been tied to the bottom of the chair so she wouldn't be able to move, run or kick at anyone who might come for her. She turned her head side to side to stretch her neck and shoulders, though the pain had grown so severe, she began to moan and grumble in agony.

It was the sense of smell that came back next, making her instantly sicker than she had ever felt. The stench of rotting flesh swirled around the room mixing with an overall smell of feces, piss and filth. An odd scent of old smoke and charcoal also came out to play along with the wretched stenches that claimed the air as their own. The air stung and burned her nose, throat and lungs as she frantically breathed in and out. Her body tried to reject the sour air as it crashed into the back of her throat. Her throat closed in on itself, forcing her to gasp to keep oxygen inside of her bloodstream. Her body recoiled as a mix of vomit and stomach bile raced up her esophagus to her mouth. With everything she had, she pushed the acidic mixture back to her guts as her head spun from the woozy feeling that overcame her and grew stronger.

Next, it was her vision, which she soon regretted. Her eyes focused on her surroundings as a house of pure horrors came to life around her. A true hell. One worse than anything she had ever imagined, read about or seen in her nightmares or the movies. Minimal, dull yellow light illuminated minor parts of the space. To her left, pure black as the light faded and was swallowed by the darkness. A blue, plastic trash can rest next to her chair. The light cut the darkness just enough for her to see what appeared to be blood soaked bones stacked inside. Scraps of flesh stuck to some of the bones that had been rotting for quite some time. At the far end of the room, a small mattress sat upon the floor pressed against the wall. It wasn't neatly made, or neat at all. It was stained and covered in filth, like the rest of the room. One solitary, crumbled, sad pillow rested against the wall as though it was weeping. A wrinkled blanket that looked like it was dragged from a dumpster laid upon the foot of the mattress.

The walls of the room were plastered with wallpaper that was bubbling, stained and tearing away from the structure. It appeared, at one time, that it was a burnt yellow color with a white floral pattern throughout. Now, much like the entirety of this space, it screamed to be torn down. Burnt, buried and forgotten. Valerie feared she was now inside one of those trailers they had seen from the parking lot. In fact, she was certain of it. Not only did she fail at escaping the monster, she was now in his home.

Just when she thought her living nightmare couldn't get worse, she turned to her right. Slowly, her head shifted to that side of the room. Her eyes burst with fear and shock as she focused on everything happening around the room. Stacked on top of one another only a few feet away were each of her friends. Limp, lifeless and soaked in blood. Each of them was covered in fatal wounds.

The bodies were piled in the order in which this maniac had killed and captured them. Almost as though the psycho had used each body as part of a collection, piling them one by one as he ran them down and killed them. When she shifted her head downward, she saw Spencer. His pale white face stuck and full of pricks from a cactus, his throat and neck slashed from collarbone to jawline. Next, her best friend Jenna. Her throat slashed with a thick, gaping wound, with flesh that dangled back into the open cavity. Her body was torn to bits as though a giant claw had ripped through her abdomen. On top of Jenna was her older brother, Brad. Seeing him in this state, only a few inches away from her own body, solidified the feelings she had tried so hard to suppress. His face and throat both eviscerated from the thrashing he had taken from this mindless killer and his meat hook. His jaw bone sat askew and hung sideways away from the rest of his skull. His eyes wide open in lasting terror. On top of the pile of bodies was good old Tom the Trucker, his abdomen sliced wide open. As she stared into the gaping hole of his body cavity, she twisted her head away, leaned over and vomited onto the floor. She cried harder than she could ever remember crying. She noticed the absence of Lexi and prayed maybe she had run to safety. Or at least escaped the fate of those on the floor.

Just then, the door to the trailer popped open with intense force. The hinges creaked and cried as the door smashed into the outside wall. Standing outside in the darkness was the madman, covered head to toe in dried and still drying crimson, with Spencer's stupid mask over his head.

He reached upwards with his right hand, grabbing onto a railing just inside the door. He grunted as he pulled himself up into the trailer, dragging his oblong body inside. Once inside, he reached out, pulling the door shut behind him. He spun his body around and stood directly in front of Valerie. He moved in frantic motions. Almost playful, like this was a game. To him, it must be. He stared at her through the mask for a moment and she could hear him taking deep breaths. Each one followed by its own grunt and wheeze.

"Oh, look at that," He said through the mask, phlegm rattling within his throat. "You did wake up. How about that?"

His voice was deep, unemotional and had a rattle to it, almost like a steel canister filled with loose gravel. Like he had been choking on phlegm for years, refusing to clear it from his old, disgusting throat.

"What do you want!" She screamed as she tried to pull her legs up to protect her body. She continued through with a stuttered speech. "Who? Who the-the fuck are you!?"

The masked maniac leaned in real close - So close she could smell the evil as it oozed from his pores. He pressed his filthy index finger into her lips.

"Shhhh," He whispered. Which sounded like a baby's rattle filled with bullets. "Don't worry your pretty head, little girl. You'll know everything soon."

He kept his finger pressed into her lips for a moment, staring deep into her terrified eyes. She watched his crossed eyes flip back and forth inside his skull from behind that mask. She was almost certain she heard him chuckling ever so slightly to himself. He pulled his finger from her lips and ran it over the gaping wound on her left cheek, drawing an invisible circle around her left eye, then running it through her long hair. He grabbed a handful of hair and jerked her head back with ferocious strength. Her head snapped backwards as she winced in pain and closed her eyes tight.

"You're a pretty one," He whispered. He forced her head to move in all directions so he could admire her features. "It'll be a real shame to ruin those good looks. But I bet you'll taste great."

When he let go, she pushed her body into the chair the best she could to gain some distance from him. He only laughed at her sad attempt to move further from him.

"Fight as much as you wish, little girl. You ain't going anywhere."

CHAPTER 27

Valerie trembled, making the chains crackle against themselves, filling the air with the sound like that of an eerie popcorn machine filled with screws. Sweat poured from her head and face, soaking through her hooded sweatshirt so much that it dripped onto the floor beneath her. She couldn't stand the sight of anything in that disgusting trailer, though she refused to take her shaking eyes off of the masked maniac. Fear brings out irrational thinking in human beings. It can make you do things you otherwise wouldn't ever dream of. She felt if she saw something coming from the madman - whatever it may be - maybe she could brace herself. She figured it pointless to brace for a hit or attack when you are chained like an abused animal. But in times of great duress, we all think and do crazy things. And if there were a time in Valerie's brief life to act irrationally, this was it.

At the far end of the trailer, just past the pile of her dead friends, sat a small kitchenette. A once cream colored yet now stain covered laminate countertop stretched the width of the room. In the center sat a stainless-steel sink and faucet that looked like it would be used in a professional kitchen, the faucet stretching high into the air. On the far left, a cutout of the counter allowed for a half-sized white refrigerator that was coated in years of stains and rust. Pressed far back against the wall was a butcher's block, loaded with different chef's knives. Next to the block was a stack of large steel mixing bowls. Just to the right of the sink was a dark gray metal contraption fashioned with a giant crank on the front and a space at the top in which users could load various food items. The man maneuvered around the kitchenette like a bumble bee escaping a fire. Bouncing back and forth from one end to the other, almost with no set plan, gathering items and utensils. Or, torture devices, one might think, depending on the day. From the block of various knives, the man snatched a large butcher's knife.

"What, um," Valerie said, clearing her nervous throat as she spoke. "What are you going to do to me? To *us*?"

The man stopped dead in his tracks as the innocent words hit his ears. He dropped the butcher's knife onto the countertop and removed Spencer's mask. His head slowly turned to her direction, when, for the very first time, she could see his horrific face. His eyeballs floating aimlessly inside his skull, sunken in like two rotting black olives. His features appeared as though they were ripped from 3 different faces to compile this one, with each area uglier than the next. A mustache sat above his upper lip, and a scar that never healed decorated the right side of his face, infected and oozing. His hair was thin and wispy and shot in all directions into the air, with a bald spot right at the front of his head.

"You're going to sit right there and wait patiently while I do my preparations," He grunted. "Tomorrow is cooking day, little girl." He turned back to the counter, picking up the large butcher's knife again.

"Cooking day?" She asked as tears raced one another down her face.

"Yes, cooking day. Would you like to see? A little demonstration, so to speak?"

She wished she hadn't asked for clarification.

He pulled his body across the room awkwardly. He moved in a way that proved his body was breaking down like an old Datsun. His body was tweaked, and his right shoulder fell towards the floor as he moved. He took a large, labored step towards her, his bad leg only dragged behind him. He moved painfully, yet the pain didn't seem to bother him. It seemed completely normal, second nature. He stood in front of the pile of bodies, took a deep breath and ran his right forearm over his lips. As he bent down, a low growl rolled out of his mouth as he shoved his hands underneath Brad's lifeless body. He began pulling and pulling, until the body dangled backwards over Spencer and Jenna's, his head and shoulders crashing onto the filthy floor. There Brad's limp body hung, stretched backwards, like a wet shirt on a clothesline.

"Let me show you," He mumbled through heavy breaths.

He lifted Brad's right arm into the air. Holding it by the limp, cold wrist, he slashed again and again at Brad's shoulder. Dull thuds of steel hitting bone, tendon and muscle echoed off the walls. Valerie closed her eyes and shrieked in shock as the heavy blade struck again and again. The man dropped the knife onto the floor, grabbed the arm at the wrist, pulling and twisting like a wishbone on Thanksgiving until it snapped off Brad's body. He grabbed the knife with his left hand, holding the arm in his right and stood to his feet.

"I overheard everything you said to this boy before I killed him," He muttered. "He's a bit of a hot head now, isn't he? Well, he was. *Was* a hot head."

Valerie's head dropped forward as her chin hit her chest. Shock was setting in. Unfortunately, she was awakened again immediately. For better or worse, she was stronger than she knew. At this moment, she prayed silently in her head for God to take her away from this hell. But here she remained. Here she was stuck. Living out a nightmare of biblical proportions.

"I think this little guy will make a perfect Hot n Spicy. Him being such a hot head, that is. What do you say?"

The man waddled back to the counter, dropped the dismembered arm onto the cutting board and slapped it a couple times with his open right palm. He grabbed the wrist with his left hand, lifting it so the finger tips pointed towards the ceiling as it rested on what was once the shoulder. He then took the butcher's knife, stuck it into the arm and slid the blade downward towards the counter. A long sheet of human flesh pulled away from the bone as he carefully sliced. He dropped the arm, which resulted in a loud thud as it fell. He held the sheet of thick human flesh into the air and admired it. He then turned to show it to Valerie.

"That there is a real beauty, little girl. You can't beat that right there."

He stuck the sliced flesh into the contraption with the crank. Holding the flesh with his left hand, he began cranking away. At the bottom of the device, with every spin, thick strips of flesh were produced and fell onto the counter top. Valerie knew then, the contraption was some sort of hand cranked meat slicer. When he finished, 4 long slices of flesh about a quarter inch thick remained. He held up a strip of Brad's skin and shook it in Valerie's direction.

"Oh yeah," He grunted, admiring the strip of meat. "That there is a beauty. Hot n Spicy it is. Hot n Spicy it shall be."

He gathered the strips and tossed them into a mixing bowl. He then pulled a stained towel from a bar that hung on the wall behind the sink and patted his hands dry.

"You see, little girl? The best meat money can buy, it needs to be fresh. Fresh meat. That's what the people want. That's what the people demand from me. And that's exactly what I give them."

He waddled his misshapen body back to Valerie, pressing his hands onto the arms of the chair. He lowered his body and crouched eye to eye with her.

"It was a real blessing you and your little friends showed up when you did. I was getting nervous I wouldn't be able to cook tomorrow. And we can't have that, little girl. No, we can't have that. You see, the people," He said, sucking in air loudly and pointing at the outside world. "The people, they're hungry little girl. And it's up to me, yes, it's up to me to feed them. OK? Boy, a real blessing you all showed up when you did. Now, the hungry people? They can feast. Oh yes, a feast."

Tears continued to rain down her cheeks, her lips quivered and quaked, and she was terrified beyond the ability to speak or think. She had stared into the eye of a hurricane of evil. A veritable devil had come to life on earth.

"It was so nice of you to find this truck driver for me. He's a little old, and his meat might be tough, yes might be tough. But he will do. He will do just fine. He can make up for your friend who fell into my pit."

She knew he meant Lexi. She knew then Lexi hadn't made it to safety after all. She wasn't alive, and no help was coming to save her. Somehow knowing she died in a pit put her at ease. She wouldn't be chopped up and served to, whomever it was he kept referring to. She didn't know, and she didn't want to.

"Please," she begged. "Please, let me go. I, I promise I won't say a word. Just, please, let me live. Let me go."

"Oh no, little girl. You're not going anywhere, no, not anywhere."

He lifted a carving knife and held it in front of his face. The blade sparkled even in the minimal light. He twisted and turned the blade in various directions as he admired it.

"You know what makes the best meat, little girl? When you get it as fresh as you can. Sometimes, yes sometimes, it's best to carve the meat directly off a live animal. A live animal's flesh and meat, you can taste the freshness. Yes, the freshness of living meat."

He placed the knife onto the top of her bare thigh, pressing the blade in ever so slightly. A small trickle of blood lifted from under the blade and began to drip down her leg. He smiled, showing a set of black, rotting teeth inside his decaying mouth. His eyes bounced back and forth as they tried to focus with hers.

"Now, close your eyes, little girl," He said. "This one's gonna hurt."

He pressed the blade deep into her thigh as he sawed and carved back and forth, cutting clean through her leg. A massive slab of flesh that was bone deep dropped onto the floor. Valerie recoiled in horrific pain, convulsing, jumping and bouncing in the chair. She tried with all of her might to pull herself from the confines of the chains, but they didn't budge. He sank the knife into the inside of her thigh and began slicing and carving downward. He then did the same to her left leg, carving all the flesh from her thighs down to the bone.

She screamed, and she screamed. Screamed until her body gave out. Screams transformed to shrill cries as all the life drained from her body. Maybe it was the blood loss. Maybe it was the shock. Maybe a bit of both. At that moment, just as the light in her eyes died, she envied the bodies that lay next to her.

And with a few quick swipes of a blade, all the hope within Valerie was gone. Like vapor from a boiling pot, it dissipated into the air almost as though it had never existed at all. The small light of hope deep within her spirit was gone. Snuffed out like a solitary candle left alone, too close to an open window during a winter storm.

CHAPTER 28

Valerie's lifeless body remained chained to that chair, as the man continued to slice away at the fresh flesh that remained on her body. Down her legs, her arms and even the sides of her abdomen, until there was nothing left that resembled a once bright, shining young woman. She once brimmed with life, her mind filled with dreams and ambitions. Now, reduced to nothing more than scraps left at the feet of a monstrous butcher. He kept her body there as he proceeded to cut each of the victims' limb from limb, slicing the meat from their bodies and bones in a similar, yet in a somehow even more careless fashion.

With Valerie he took his time. His cuts were precise. Slow, thought out and with intention. For the bodies stacked on the floor of his trailer of horrors, he showed no care. No concern. He sliced and diced them in such an animalistic fashion, that when he tore unabashedly at one of Jenna's arms, he tore it clear off her body.

"Hello there," He said with a devilish laugh, waving the disembodied hand in front of Valerie's lifeless face. He pushed the flopping arm towards her, so that the fingers brushed against her pale, ice cold cheek. "Wake up. Oh, don't be dead. What will I do without you?" He continued to laugh at their expense.

He opened the door to the trailer, allowing the fresh air to pour in and mix with the rotting stench of death that lived in all corners of the condemnable trailer. On the sand below, just before the steps to crawl in, was a worn-out wheelbarrow. He tossed Brad's arm out of the trailer, as it flopped around with a loud thud. Then, he knelt down, shoved his hands under one body, painfully stood to his feet - grunting and panting as he went. He dragged Tom the Trucker's shredded skeleton to the door, down the steps and placed the body into the wheelbarrow, his face lifelessly staring towards the starry sky. One by one, he wrestled each body down the steps, placing each one on top of the others into the squeaky wheelbarrow. He reentered the trailer, knelt down and grabbed Jenna by her bloody sweatshirt. The sweatshirt had become soaked in crimson liquid and had since hardened around her body. Pulling at the sweatshirt, he hoisted Jenna's ice cold, hardening body over his right shoulder. Her head and remaining arm dangling and swaying behind his back as he turned towards the door. He bent, tossing her body without care onto the pile just outside the door.

He stepped down and wiped his lips with his sleeve. The sleeve of his long-sleeve shirt was stained with years of filth, blood and many other bodily fluids that no one would ever want to encounter. He reached for the handles of the wheelbarrow, muscled them upwards as he pushed it across the sand. At a snail's pace, he pushed the heavy, literal dead weight, one small inch at a time until he reached the lip of the pit. He dropped the back end, took a deep breath and again, wiped his quivering, misshapen lips. After a few breaths, he lifted the handles again, this time, positioning his hands underneath as to tilt the cart enough that the contents would dump out.

One by one, the dead, chopped and carved bodies fell into the burn pit. Bones cracked and flesh thudded as they settled in a sort of knot. A knot tied and twisted of human appendages and limbs. He pulled a matchbook from the back pocket of his filth covered pants, striking it against his coarse butcher's smock. The match hissed as it caught fire, the flame flickering and dancing in the darkness, as one solitary plume of smoke lifted into the air, like a ballerina twirling on stage surrounded by stage lights.

As he dropped the lit match into the pit, a loud swoosh filled the silence as everything inside was swallowed by the explosive flames. He admired the flames for a while, outstretching his hands towards the warmth. He rubbed them together over the growing flame to warm his joints and fingers.

When he returned inside, he found himself standing before many baking sheets, each one covered in large slabs of meat. Human flesh that he himself cut and butchered off the dead - and in one case, still living - bodies of his victims. He lifted one tray and made his way to the counter next to the sink. He lifted a big hunk of meat that resembled the outside of a person's thigh. He slapped it onto the counter, and patted it twice with his open, bare palms. Lifting a sharp carving knife, he carefully slid it forward, then pulled it back towards him, sinking the blade deeper and deeper as he went. When one slice fell off, he continued the maneuver until the hunk of meat had been transformed into slices. He lifted each slice, and lowered them into his countertop meat slicer. He cranked away at that metal grinder, as the long, thick slice was transformed into 6 half-inch thick slices.

He continued this for every piece of disembodied flesh he had collected from the visitors - his victims - until he had trays upon trays of somewhat uniformed slices of flesh. It took hours for him to prepare every inch of the meat he had acquired. It was funny to him just how quickly he could take a life, only for the preparation to slow him down for hours, and sometimes days. But to him, it was all part of his process. Besides, this was nothing new to him. This was his job. And clearly, he was thriving.

He stacked baking sheets about 6 high - each filled with long, half-inch thick by 4-inch long strips of meat - and loaded them onto his trusty wheelbarrow. He pushed it through the sand, and around the back of the three trailers. He stopped at the middle trailer, setting the cart down. After removing a small gold key from his back pocket, the man sunk it into a gold lock and pulled the two doors wide open. The trailer was a repurposed shipping container, and inside he had it set up like a prep kitchen.

On the left side were stainless steel shelves stretching from front to back, each filled with numerous tubs of spices, seasonings and liquid marinade bottles. To the right, beyond the doors sat a giant steel kitchen table. On the shelf under the table top were countless steel bowls stacked perfectly. Just beyond the table were four full sized refrigerators, all in a row.

It took a few trips, but, he made his way with the last wheelbarrow loaded with baking sheets of fresh cut flesh. Each load, he carried into the prep station, stacking the sheets on the metal shelves to the left. He then reached under the table and pulled out a stack of bowls. In one bowl, he poured in a heavy dose of soy sauce, brown sugar, ginger, garlic, honey, sesame oil and rice vinegar. With a slotted spoon, he stirred the contents together until it thickened. He began dropping strands of meat into the mixture, tossing about a dozen in the thick brown liquid until covered. After the meat was removed from the bowl, one at a time, he replaced them onto a baking sheet, continuing the process for a few of the trays filled with meat. Then, each tray was safely stored inside one of the fridges along the wall.

In the next bowl, he reached for the seasoning shelf to add copious amounts of red chili paste, honey, minced, fresh ginger and some lime juice. Then, he grated fresh garlic over the mixture, topping it off with a splash or two of soy sauce. He returned to the sheets of meat, scouring them as though he was searching for some specific slices.

"Where are you," He muttered to himself over and over. "Ah, there you are. Mr. Hot Head. Mr. Tough Guy. Mr. Hero of the Day! You, Mr. Hot Head, you get to be hot and spicy."

He tipped the baking sheet to one side, spilling multiple strips of pink, sliced meat into the bowl and marinade. With a few tosses by his bare hands, he lifted each slice onto its own sheet, and into the fridge for cooling.

In two more large bowls, he mixed together ingredients for two more marinades. In one, he emptied two store bought bottles of Italian dressing, a bottle of spicy BBQ sauce, finishing it with some salt and pepper. In the last bowl, he mixed olive oil, fresh lemon juice, a sprinkle of salt, a splash of water and a couple of heaping spoons full of mesquite seasoning.

"There we go," He said through throaty, deep breaths. "Sweet and savory and mesquite." He dipped his index finger into the mesquite marinade, lifting it to his mouth. He shoved his finger in deep, sucking all the savory liquid from his discolored fingertip. "Perfection," he whispered.

The remaining meat strips went into the two bowls to marinate, before being placed in one of the refrigerators to stay cool, and for the flavors to soak into the meat. He took pride in his preparation space, as he cleaned the entire area until it was spotless. He put everything back in its rightful place, he slammed the doors shut, replacing the padlock.

CHAPTER 29

The next afternoon...

The sun hung high over the California desert, burning everything in sight with its powerful, booming rays. A few scattered clouds were painted across the bright blue sky, resembling cotton balls that had been stretched beyond recognition. Wisps of white streaks with subtle hints of gray and silver underneath and throughout.

On a rock that sat buried deep into the sand, just off the road, was a lizard. Its eyes closed and its head poked upwards as it basked in the hot sunshine beating down upon the earth. There, the innocent lizard sunbathed without a care in the world. Even the buzzards hovering overhead couldn't phase the little lizard. Besides, the buzzards had something else in mind. And that something else happened to be occurring at the trailers in the distance. The house of horrors where just a few hours prior, hell had visited earth. The buzzards knew flesh was about. They knew where it was. If only they could get to it.

From down the road, a highway patrol car came into sight as it moved towards the abandoned parking lot. It passed the rock, scaring our lizard friend from its afternoon sunbathing session. The lizard stutter stepped for a moment, before it scurried underneath the rock and into the shade. Humans always show up and disrupt wildlife. The true trespassers on this planet.

The highway patrol car turned into the parking lot and came to a stop in the spot next to the Zeus the teenage travelers had left behind. As the engine came to a dead stop, both the driver and passenger doors flung open. The driver was Officer Steve Tomkins. A veteran of the California Highway Patrol. He wore a long-sleeved, tan police uniform shirt, tucked neatly into a pair of matching tan police officer slacks. Thick and heavy boots covered his feet, and a pair of dark aviators covered his eyes from the encroaching sun. His face showed his age - What one would assume in his early 50s - and the hair remaining on his head and above his upper lip did the same. Both washed over in differing tones of gray.

From the passenger side, Officer Kevin Wiley stepped onto the asphalt. Officer Wiley was a recruit with the Highway Patrol, running around on a ride-along with some of the veterans until he could dive in on his own. A young recruit in his early 20s, he had a buzzed haircut, clean-shaven face and was built like a football player. Thick arms and chest burst through his tan, short-sleeved patrol uniform. A pair of sunglasses that resembled Officer Tomkins protected his eyes from the blazing sun.

"Well, I think we can say we found the stolen car, huh Kev?" Tomkins said, running his right hand over the top of his head.

"It would appear that way, sir," Wiley replied, trying his best to sound confident. Like he thought a cop should. "Should I radio this in?"

"No hurry," Tomkins replied. "We'll get to that in due time."

"But, isn't that man from San Francisco looking for the car? Shouldn't we let him know?"

"Make him sweat it out," He said, taking a few steps towards the edge of the lot.

He passed by Officer Wiley as he made his way to the sand, lowering his glasses on his nose and watched those trailers in the distance.

He continued, "Rich city folk like him, well, I've got no sympathy for people like him." He pulled his sunglasses down further to the tip of his nose as he turned back towards the young officer. "In other words, fuck him."

They both shared a friendly laugh.

"Say," Wiley said, meeting the veteran officer at the edge of the parking lot. "What do you think is going on out there, huh? By those old, abandoned trailers?"

From behind the trailers, huge plumes of thick, white smoke shot up into the air, swirling and dancing as they rose higher and higher, until they became so thin, they disappeared in the warm, desert breeze. The surrounding air, as faint as it was, smelled delicious. Different smells of sweet, rich BBQ and fire cooked meat surrounded them, even at that distance.

"Oh that? You mean all that smoke?" Asked Tomkins, pulling his belt and adjusting his pants. "Well Wiley, you're about to experience something real special. Something you may not even be able to believe or understand. You like BBQ, son?"

"Of course," He said with a smirk and a condescending tone. "Who doesn't?"

"You'd be surprised how many pussified cops I've had the displeasure of working with in my career, son. Glad to hear you enjoy some good old fashioned, American meat."

"My favorite, sir," He confirmed. "One of my favorite pastimes, too. I love cooking over a flame with my Pops. It's something he taught me young, and I still do it every chance I get for my family. I can't wait to teach my boy how to handle a grill."

"That's the spirit, Kev," He said with a pat on the shoulder. "You make me more and more proud every day we work together. But let me tell ya, what you're about to try is *really* going to blow your mind."

Just then, Officer Tomkins put his fingers to his lips, inhaled deep and let out all the breath, resulting in an ear-piercing whistle. The whistle was so loud, it sounded like it bounced off the clouds and the mountains as it flew through the open air. As the whistle rattled about, just before it lost all momentum and died, the door of the closest trailer shot wide open. It had been pushed so hard, it banged against the outside wall of the trailer, bouncing about in the breeze.

One step, followed by another came the maniac from the night before, his awkward face out in the open on full volume. Somehow, he was more terrifying in the daylight. His facial features appeared to have almost melted together, creating an abstract look. His nose sort of merged with his lips, and deep, sunken eyes that couldn't focus on any one thing at a time seemed almost two inches further apart than anyone the officers had ever seen. He slowly dragged his overweight, chubby body through the sand towards the officers. His shoulder shot downward at the ground, and in his left hand he held a plastic grocery store bag.

"Holy shit," Wilky whispered, taking a step or two back away as the man approached.

"Chill out, son," Tomkins said, reaching back with his right hand to calm his nerves. "He's alright. And *you'll* be alright. He moves a bit slow, and he's pretty freaky looking. But he's a good guy. And if you stay on his good side, you'll get a lot of tasty treats from him. So, remember that."

"Jesus," The young officer whispered in shock. "I can't even tell what would *be* his good side."

"Don't be disrespectful, son," The veteran shot back. "If you act like a dickhead, I won't share with you."

"Share what?"

"Oh, you'll see."

After a long period had passed, the man reached the officers.

"Good afternoon, Officers," The man grunted through a phlegm filled throat. "How can I help you gentlemen today?"

"Good Afternoon, Mr. Herkey," Tomkins said. "We're out on patrol looking for a stolen car from San Francisco."

"San Francisco, huh?" Herkey asked. His voice, shaky and disgusting. "These big city folks trying to get a piece of the ol' desert, huh?"

"Something like that," Tomkins said. "Turns out this is the car right back here. Guess we'll be calling it in."

"That one there, you say? Must've stopped to, uh, must've stopped to get a charge I would say."

"Sure seems that way, Mr. Herkey. Say, you didn't happen to see anyone hanging around here last night or this morning, did you?"

"Nope," He said, lying through his charcoal black teeth. "Can't say that I have."

"Figures. Someone must've used your parking lot as a dump space. Someone probably picked the thief up. Probably half drunk at a black jack table in Caesar's Palace by now."

"You know them city folk and their money, huh officer?" Herkey said with a laugh.

"Sure do," He said, returning a laugh. "Bunch of idiots, throwing money away at a casino."

"Fucking idiots," Wilke chimed in.

"So. Who's the youngin you got with you, Officer?" Herkey asked. His eyes were floating around between the two of them. Kevin couldn't tell if he was looking at him, Officer Tomkins, or something else altogether. Either way, he was rightfully freaked.

"This young buck right here," Officer Wilke said, wrapping his right arm around the young Officer's shoulders. "This is my latest recruit. My new partner you could say, ain't that right?" He shook Kevin.

"That's right, sir," Kevin said with a loose smile. "The name is Kevin. Kevin Wiley. Pleasure to meet you, sir."

"No need to call me sir, Officer. You can call me Herkey. That's how I'm known around these parts."

The two shared an awkward handshake, as Herkey's eyes continued to float around in his skull, like two golf balls that had fallen into a swimming pool.

"These parts, huh?" The young Officer asked with a raised brow. "Say, do you mind me asking what it is you're doing out here all by yourself?"

"Come on now, Kev," Officer Wilkens said, a sense of annoyance in his voice. "No need to grill Mr. Herkey about what he's up to. He's an upstanding citizen in my book."

"It's fine to ask. I don't mind," Herkey said, taking a stutter step forward. He then turned to his left, glancing over his left shoulder out at the emptiness of the desert. "All this land, well, it's all mine. All mine."

"Wow, you own all of this?"

"Sure do. My father ran that there garage and general store for years before he invested in my business. That's when he retired, so to speak.

Let's just say, he helped me out with the first batch of my now world-famous jerky. And the rest, well, that's history."

"And you built a parking lot? All the way out here? In the middle of nowhere?"

"Sure did. Well, I didn't build it. Some tech company from the big city came in and built it. Paid me a pretty penny to take up the land too, you see?"

"These big tech companies are moving into the country and installing these charging stations for the rich and elite to charge their electric vehicles when they travel," The Veteran Officer chimed in. "Those prissy cars can't make it from one destination to the next without a boost of energy."

"Your partner is correct," Herkey said with a creepy wink. "They paid me quite handsomely to put it out here on my land. I don't mind. No one ever bothers me while they're here, and it pays me to grow my business."

"Say," Officer Wilkens jumped in. "How is the business going? You still using that big city money to build your farm?"

"Oh, you're building a full-fledged farm, huh?" The young Officer asked.

"Sure am. It's going to be a site to behold, let me tell ya. We're building it up by Primm, on the state line. It's going to be beautiful. Carnival rides for the kiddies. A big restaurant with fresh food from the farm. A real destination. And can ya believe it? A full ranch resort built from big city tech and jerky money."

"Can't beat country folk," Officer Wilkens said.

"Ain't that the truth."

"Say, speaking of the business. What have you got for us today?" Wilkens asked, rubbing his palms together.

"I got some fresh meat for you, just took it off the smoker. It's cooled and ready to eat. Here you go, I already packed it up for the both of you," Herkey said, handing the Veteran Officer the large, plastic bag. The plastic handles tied in a perfect little knot on top.

The elder officer untied the bag as though the secret to life was hidden inside. He sank his nose in, taking in a deep sniff filling his nostrils with the smell of sweet, smokey meat. As his head emerged, his eyes were closed while an ear to ear grin wrapped his eager face. He was in heaven.

"Ahh," He let out as he exhaled. "These trips out to the desert, Mr. Herkey. You always make it *so* worth it."

He reached into the bag to retrieve a smaller bag that had been vacuum sealed. Inside were a handful of marinated, smoked strips of fresh meat. He set the main bag at his feet before he began tearing away at the smaller one.

"I see you've chosen the sweet and savory as your first taste, huh, Officer?"

"It's my favorite!" He shouted like a child who had been allowed to eat cake for breakfast.

"So, wait," The younger Officer said as a confused look washed over his face. "That's what you do all the way out here? Make beef jerky?"

"Pretty much," Herkey said with a smile. "It's my land. Who can tell me what to do out here?"

"Take a piece, Wiley," Wilkens held the bag towards his young partner. "Now, tell me that isn't the best jerky you've ever eaten in your brief life."

He reached his right index finger and thumb into the bag, pulling out a long strip of meat. He held it in the air as he admired it. It was charred and incredibly moist. Moister than any jerky he had ever touched. He figured it was because he hadn't ever eaten jerky as fresh as this. He shoved the strip into his mouth and clamped down with his teeth, pulling and tearing at the strip until a morsel broke off and fell onto his tongue. As he chewed the morsel, it almost liquified between his teeth. His mouth caught fire with a mélange of flavors from sweet molasses, savory spices and a perfect hint of fresh smoke and wood.

"Holy. Wow, *damn* that is magnificent," The young cop said as he chewed.

"You see what I mean, son?" The older cop said as he tore at his own strip of fresh meat. His mouth also filled with the delightful flavors of sweet and savory as the meat broke down and melted in his mouth.

"You've certainly outdone yourself this time, Herkey," The cop said. "I really don't understand how you do it."

"I've got my own special technique, you could say. It helps to keep the meat as fresh as possible until it's cooked. This specific batch you're enjoying came from a real beauty named Valerie. Gorgeous animal. Very sweet, yet savory enough for my liking."

"Wait," Wiley interjected with confusion. "Do you name the cows you butcher? And you season the meat based on their personalities? Isn't that, I don't know, kind of creepy, Mr. Herkey?"

"Don't question my methods, young man," Herkey said. His face was tight with anger as he glared straight through the young man's body. "Or there will be no more meat for you."

"You heard him, Wiley. Don't ruin the freebies for me. I look forward to this jerky anytime I come out here. Why don't you go call a tow truck to come get this car, huh? Make yourself useful. Let the adults catch up."

"Sure thing, sir," Wiley said, taking a few steps away from the older men. "Sir, I didn't mean any disrespect. I swear."

"No apologies needed, young man," Herkey said. The clear anger still fresh on his distorted face. "There will be plenty of meat for everyone, yourself included. Maybe one day you can help me make a batch."

"That would be my honor, sir," Wiley said. He nodded and turned his back to them. He pulled his radio and called in the abandoned car to be transported back to the small town of Baker.

CHAPTER 30

The next morning Mr. and Mrs. Miller had risen with the sun. Mr. Miller couldn't - and wouldn't - wait another minute to get his precious, prized vehicle back in his possession. Before the mist and fog of night had burned away and been replaced with warming rays from the California sky, they had rushed out the front door of their hill-top estate and made their way out of town. Mrs. Miller was less interested in the car's return, knowing full and well it would be fine. And even if something happened to his precious vehicle, she knew her husband had the money - and determination for better or worse - to replace it. But, what couldn't be replaced in her mind and heart, were her children. She continued to go through the motions for them. The kids. In her mind, one of them had to care about the well-being of their babies. And it had been made clear over the years that it wouldn't be her husband.

"I hate driving your car," Mr. Miller barked as he adjusted his position in the driver seat.

Mr. Miller looked as though he was on his way to play a round of golf. Dark gray athletic pants, a matching polyester track style jacket with a white and black striped polo shirt underneath. The collar of the polo had been pulled up and out to showcase itself and folded over the neck of the jacket. A white dad style hat sat on his head. He pulled at the seat belt, pressed his feet into the floorboard and lifted his ass off the seat repeatedly attempting to get comfortable. She was none too surprised by his outbursts, as she had grown all too familiar with his childishness throughout the years. It wasn't as though Mrs. Miller drove around town in an old, rundown vehicle that should be taken out behind a barn and put out of its misery. Mr. Miller would never have that. Partially because he did in fact spoil his wife. Though it was all about image to Mr. Miller. Her image reflected on him, or so he believed. He wanted his wife to look good at all times. From cocktail parties, to sitting poolside and yes, even when driving around town. Cars, clothes and houses were status symbols to him. Down to how his family carried themselves in public. In his mind, these things mattered.

"Quit being such a baby," Mrs. Miller barked back. She sat low in the passenger seat, chewing a mouthful of gum, flicking through her cell phone.

Tammy Miller wore a pink velour suit with huge tortoise shell sunglasses hiding her eyes from the world and a dad style San Francisco Giants hat that covered her styled blonde hair. Her oversized cell phone was covered in a shiny, gold case with thousands of fake crystals resembling diamonds. From the phone case hung a dangly charm of a champagne glass.

"It's just so uncomfortable. I can't get comfortable in this stupid car. We never should've bought this behemoth."

"Well, you never have to drive it, now do you? So get over it. I offered to drive today, didn't I?"

"A man drives his woman. That's how this works," He said as he turned his head, burning a hole through her body with his intense glare. "Can you imagine if people saw me being courted around town by a woman?"

"OK, Thomas. You made your point," she said with a roll of the eyes and smacking her gum at him. "How many times do I have to tell you to slow down? You're driving way too fast."

"Stop it. You want to get to the kids, don't you?"

"Yes, of course. But I would like to do it in one piece."

"Well, calm down and I'll get us there. Besides, I want to get to that car before something happens to it. Oh god, if they did anything to that car. They're going to have hell to pay."

"I can't believe you are more worried about that stupid car than your own children. It's very disappointing."

"How can you even say that to me? Of course, I care about the kids. But Brad and Jenna and basically adults, Tammy. They can take care of themselves. Shit, Jenna has been telling you that since middle school. Just because you refuse to believe it doesn't make it any less true," He began shuffling his position again. "That car can't take care of itself. It needs someone, *like me*, to ensure it's a well-oiled machine."

"You're pathetic, Thomas," she said, continuing to flick through her phone and smack her lips. "And for the last fucking time, slow down."

They continued to blaze down the freeway, leaving the big city in the rear-view mirror as they entered the dry air of the California desert. They had just seen road signs declaring they were about to hit Bakersfield when Mr. Miller's phone rang in his pants pocket.

"Shit," He shouted as he shuffled in his seat. He held his right hand in the air ready to accept the call so it would play through the car speakers. "How do I answer this call? Tammy, come on! How do I answer the call?"

"You're not connected to this car, Thomas. It's a phone. Just answer it like you answer every other phone that ever existed."

He leaned to his left, reached into the right pocket and pulled out his phone. He swiped his finger across the screen and placed it to the side of his head.

"Yeah? Hello? This is Thomas Miller."

"Mr. Miller? Yes, this is Officer Pullman. Is everything OK?"

"Yes, yes. Of course. I'm just fighting with my phone. I can't—"

Just then, Tammy reached over and began flipping through their satellite radio channels. Song after song rang out through the speakers as she tried to find a channel that suited her.

"Can you fucking stop?" He blurted out, holding the phone away from his face.

Mrs. Miller just waved him off, continued to chew her gum loudly and returned to the glow of her cell phone.

"Excuse me, sir?" Pullman asked.

"Not you. No, sorry. We're in the car. What can I do for you, officer?"

"Oh, you already left town? Well, then this news should please you."

"What's that?"

"Your car has been found. It was abandoned in a small parking lot in the middle of nowhere. The battery was completely dead. It's been towed to the town I mentioned when we last spoke. Baker."

"Hun, they found the car!" He blurted out.

"Did they find the kids?"

Mr. Miller rolled his eyes and waved her question away, like it was a pestering fly in his face.

"That's great news, Officer. Thank you. We're actually just entering Bakersfield. How far is Baker from here?"

"Well, Um," The officer stalled. "I'm not sure, Mr. Miller. You're going to have to do some of that leg work on your own, I'm afraid."

"Yeah, yeah. No problem. No problem at all."

"Did they find the kids?" Tammy whispered.

Again, he waved her off.

"Hey, did they find the fucking kids?" She asked again. This time, her volume was much louder.

"Did they Um, did they find the kids?"

"No sir. I appreciate you asking, but no. The kids were not with the vehicle. We have an all-points bulletin out and if any officer finds them, we will let you know right away. But be assured, the right people are looking."

"Yeah, yeah. That's fine. Look, I'm sure they made their way to Vegas already and we'll be hearing from them anytime."

"Right," Officer Pullman said with a disappointing sigh. "What you're looking for is at a gas station in Baker. It's the first gas station as you exit the freeway in town. You can't miss it."

"Thank you, officer. I appreciate it."

Thomas quickly ended the call and shoved the phone back into his pants pocket.

"Car has been found safe. It's in that shithole town, Baker. At some gas station. I guess it got towed there after they found it abandoned."

"No word on the kids and their friends?"

"Nope," He said matter-of-factly. "I'm sure they're partying in Vegas and they're doing just fine."

"If you say so," she said, reaching and turning the radio on again. This time, she settled on a Tom Petty station.

"You know, when I'm on the phone, maybe don't turn the fucking radio on."

"When you have your precious car back, you can make the rules. Until then," she said, settling back into her seat. "Fuck off."

CHAPTER 31

As the desert sun hung high in the sky parching everything in sight, Herkey was deep in his work. His old Jeep had been parked out back behind the trailers. Soon, he emerged from the furthest trailer with a red gas can dangling from his right hand. The gas inside sloshed front to back and side to side as he moved. Stumbling over his own awkward feet, as he stood at the back of the Jeep, he removed the gas cap, dropping it into his pocket as he shoved the yellow, dirt stained hose deep into the gas tank. Lifting the can upwards, gas began trickling and streaming down the hose and into the tank of the vehicle. He held it there for a moment until the stream grew silent. He tilted the can higher, hoping to drain every last drop. When the can was drained bone dry, he tossed the empty canister on the front seat of the vehicle.

Inside the middle storage container, where his kitchen had been constructed, sat 5 large storage bins sprawled across the floor. A stack of clear plastic tubs with dark blue lids that snapped into place over the side of the containers. Each container was filled top to bottom with vacuum sealed plastic bags packed tightly with fresh jerky. Written on the blue tops in black marker in giant, capital letters were each of the different flavors he produced. The fifth container had the words "EXTRA" scribbled across the top, for some overflow of each flavor, as well as some miscellaneous items.

He picked up the first container which sat closest to the open doors and wriggled his body towards the back of the Jeep. The hatch was wide open, and he began wrestling with the heavy, bulky container to get it up and into the back, followed by the other four. A tiresome job for many, especially for Old Man Herkey. His body had seen and lived through many a better day. After the containers had been shoved into the vehicle, Herkey placed a pop-up tent and a large, white, folding table into the back next to the containers of meat.

He slammed the hatch closed, took a few hard steps back and rubbed his brow of the sweat that had built up just above his eyes. He took a few deep breaths to fill his lungs with oxygen before making his way to the front of the car. The rusty door squealed as it opened, and the shocks squeaked and cracked at the weight of his large body landing into the driver side chair. He slammed the car door shut, turned the key as the ignition coughed and chugged before turning over. Dropping the gear into drive, the Jeep thrusted forward like it was an amusement park ride, before catching and allowing Herkey to drive.

The Jeep emerged from behind the trailers, bouncing up and down through the sand before it finally hit the pavement of the parking lot. At the far edge of the lot, Herkey turned right, followed by a quick left and he was on the main road towards the I-15 freeway. A slight turn to the right, and the Herkey shot up the ramp while continuing to pick up speed hoping to match the moving traffic of travelers and big rig drivers.

It wasn't a long drive to the border of California and Nevada, only about 25 minutes, give or take depending on traffic conditions, from the plain plot of land Herkey called home. Situated right along the border of the two states was the small and bustling city of Primm, Nevada.

Primm has been a popular destination spot for travelers to and from Las Vegas for decades. Not only because it was one of the few areas along that stretch of road with any signs of life, also it was the first, or last, stop for last minute indulgence of gambling, buffets and shopping at its sprawling outlet mall. One of the other claims to fame, Primm is the home to a couple of old-fashioned style casinos and hotels that are much more affordable to the general traveler than the increasing high prices of Las

Vegas. Primm was also the home of the Bonnie and Clyde murder car, where the two infamous outlaws met their maker in 1934. But the latest big ticket event in Primm was a weekly Farmer's Market that took place in the parking lot of the once bustling Buffalo Bill's Hotel and Casino.

People from all over California and Nevada came out to the massive market to sell their homemade goods, arts and crafts, fruits and vegetables, candles and any other weird and wild item your imagination could dream of. From dream catchers to date jam, kettle corn to fresh cooked corn dogs, anything money could buy could be found at the Primm Farmer's Market. Including freshly smoked and packaged Herkey's Jerky.

Herkey pulled his Jeep into the parking lot and parked in his typical market position. About once a month Herkey made the drive to Primm to peddle his meat, when supply allowed, that is. Today, he found himself again between the same two sellers as every other trip he had made.

To the right was Annie. An older woman who sold religious items including prayer candles, cross necklaces, bookmarks with scripture printed on them and even hand knitted sweaters with birds, crosses and biblical phrases stitched in. To the left was the father and son team of Frank and Franky Jr. They were mainstays at the Primm Farmer's Market, selling some of the freshest fruits and vegetables money could buy in the desert. They owned and operated a community garden closer to Las Vegas, and supplied restaurants with locally grown, pesticide free, organic produce. It was Frank's amazing jalapenos that Herkey used in his Hot n Spicy marinade.

Herkey put the Jeep in park before turning the key to stop the coughing engine from sputtering. He opened the door and stepped onto the blazing hot blacktop below.

"Mr. Herkey," Frank Senior yelled as he exited the vehicle. "What a delight. We haven't seen you in a couple of weeks, partner."

"Yeah, I know," Herkey grumbled as he maneuvered to the back of the Jeep. He pulled at the hatch and it began creaking as it opened. "Product has been slow coming. But, we're all stocked up today."

"Hey, that's great news. Say, you've got any of that Hot n Spicy or Mesquite with you? Cause boy, let me tell you, I've been craving it with a fierce hunger."

"Don't you worry your big ol' cowboy hat wearing head, Franky. I've got you covered, my friend," Herkey said through a heavy breath as he began wrestling the containers to the ground. "Good to see you, Ms. Annie. Still peddling those religious artifacts, huh, sweetheart?"

"I sell the passion and creativity that the good Lord above has blessed me with, you know that," Annie said with a laugh.

She made her way towards Herkey with her arms wide open. When she reached Herkey, she wrapped them around his bulbous body as he wrapped the arm that still worked around her waist.

"It's good to see you. How have you been?" She asked with a bright smile on her face.

"Can't complain. Besides, who would listen? Am I right?"

"Oh you," she laughed with a swat of her right hand. "Good luck today, hun. Hope you make a lot of money."

"Yeah, yeah. You too, Annie."

Herkey used every bit of his energy as he fought those heavy containers onto the blacktop. Then, he set up the pop-up tent, positioned the folding table under it and prepared a display of his freshest batch of meat for customers to sample and purchase. Small silver buckets were lined across the white table, and inside were bags of each flavor, with a handwritten sign poking out of the bucket to display what each were. Every bag was vacuum sealed, resembling something that could be sold in a store, and each had a colorful sticker with the name Herkey's Jerky and a little drawn character of himself. Next, he opened a bag of each flavor, sliced the strips inside into small, palatable bites, and set them on clean, stark white plates as free samples. When all was set up, he took a seat behind the table, wiped the sweat from his brow and took a deep breath of the hot, dry Nevada air. He was open for business.

Soon the parking lot was teaming with people, like a bee hive that had been turned over onto itself. Word had spread about the mysterious jerky, and everyone wanted to try a bite. His table was overrun with people from all walks of life hoping to sample and purchase the smokey morsels of fresh meat. A little boy who couldn't have been more than 7-years-old snapped up a sample of the teriyaki and chewed it rudely with his mouth open. He then grabbed a second cut of meat and handed it to his mother.

"Mommy, try this! It's so good. Can we buy some, please?"

"Whoa there, tiger," The boy's mom said. "We shouldn't eat a lot of beef jerky. It really isn't good for you."

"Um, excuse me, Ma'am," Herkey belted out. His voice shook like a tool chest full of loose screws. "Pardon my interruption. But, I'll have you know, my homemade jerky is as fresh as it gets. There are no preservatives, no additives and each bag is completely natural. The freshest meat you can buy. And great for growing boys' muscles."

"You hear that Mom? It's good for me. Can I get some, please?"

"All natural, huh?" She asked, her eyes surveying each bag that sat inside the silver buckets. "Well, why not? It's OK to indulge once in a while. Which one do you want, Bobby?"

"I want," He thought to himself for a moment. "This one, and, *this* one!"

"Teriyaki and Hot n Spicy for a strong, growing boy," Herkey said in a rumbling tone, like a thunderstorm rolling over the horizon. "Let me get a bag for you."

"Oh, no bag needed, thanks. We can carry these just fine."

"Even better."

She handed him a fresh, crisp $20 bill and told him to keep the change. Herkey thanked her and the little boy for their purchase.

Over the matter of a few hours, Herkey had sold every last bag of jerky that had been packaged for the market. As the sun went to sleep behind the mountains in the distance, Herkey began shoving the storage bins, pop up tent and folding table back into the Jeep. As he walked to the front of the vehicle, he noticed Frank Sr. packing up their stand as well.

"Hey, Franky," He shouted, tossing two bags of jerky his way. "They're on me, pal."

"Thanks, buddy! I appreciate it. Say, you need any fresh jalapenos?"

"I'm all set, Frank," He shouted as he slammed the heavy, squeaky door. "Next time. Next time."

Herkey left the parking lot and made his way to the main road out of town. As the sun dipped behind the desert mountains, the old, janky Jeep dipped down the on-ramp, headed back to Halloran Summit Road.

CHAPTER 32

The once bright and shiny gold Range Rover was now covered front to back and top to bottom in dust and sand from what seemed like a never-ending drive. A constant onslaught of wind and dirt had muted the paint as it blustered around them. They had finally reached the small town of Baker. Mr. Miller veered the car to the right as they exited the freeway, and followed the road as it rose and turned to the left, maneuvering over the speeding cars on the freeway below. The road straightened and dipped down as they entered onto the main thoroughfare for the small, desert town. And there it was, just like Officer Pullman had said. The gas station on the left-hand side of the road. At the far end of the parking lot, tucked back behind the mini mart, Mr. Miller could see what appeared to be his precious Zeus.

"Ah, my baby," He said, turning the wheel and pulling into the gas station lot. "There she is."

He was so eager to get to his precious car, that he didn't slow his speed much, if at all, before entering the gas station lot. The Range Rover dropped and bounced like a roller coaster ride that was out of control, sending both of them up and out of their seats.

"My god, Thomas," Tammy shouted. "Slow down. You're going to kill us or someone else."

"Oh calm down, no I'm not."

Once the SUV settled, he pressed on the gas and rushed to the back of the parking lot. Sitting at the edge of the asphalt right where it met with the sandy floor was his prized possession. Parked, safe, in front of a pair of electric vehicle charging stations. The same charging stations Brad attempted to use days before. He parked the dusty Range Rover next to the Zeus and turned off the engine as quickly as he was able. He pushed the door open and jumped out like a kid landing on the bottom step on Christmas morning. Tammy followed behind with much less enthusiasm.

"There she is!" He belted out, both arms held outward as though he could actually hug a car.

"Yup, there she is. Are you happy now?"

"Yes, I am happy now. Thank you for understanding."

"You're lucky you didn't kill someone pulling in. You were driving like an asshole."

"Shut up, I was not. Besides, look at this place. It's like hell opened up and dumped everything it didn't want out of itself. That is what Baker means to me. If I had hit someone, I'd have done them a favor."

"Whatever you say," she said under her breath.

He pulled a key fob from his back pocket, unlocked the car and pulled open the driver side door. Falling hard, he dropped himself into the front seat and kicked his legs in and under the steering wheel.

"Let's take a look at her, huh," He said, examining the interior. "They left a bit of a mess in here. Dammit, they should know better than to eat food in this thing."

He rubbed his hands over the wheel, admired for a moment and then pressed the ignition switch. Nothing happened.

"Son of a bitch," He shouted. "They couldn't at least plug her in before we arrived?"

"It's not their job to take care of your car, Thomas. You're lucky they even towed it somewhere safe for you to pick up. What do they care?"

"Fucking peasants," He grunted, lifting himself up and out of the car. "Luckily they have charging stations here. I'll charge her up and we can hit the road."

"Are we heading to Las Vegas to find the kids?"

"Vegas? No," He replied with a shake of the head and a condescending laugh. "Once she's charged up, I'm heading back home. The kids are *fine*, trust me. They're having a blast at that concert. Quit worrying about them. When they get home, we'll have plenty of time to punish them for this."

"It's just, odd," Tammy said, her left hand planted on her hip as her right rested on her forehead. "I've called them, texted them. And I still haven't received a single reply."

"They're teenagers, hun. This is what they do. They ignore their parents. Besides, if you called me while I was at a concert, I wouldn't pick up, either."

"Well, you're a jerk off. That's why."

Thomas shrugged at the insult and pulled the charging dock away from the stand-up station and stretched the hose so that it would reach the charging port on the Zeus. He then tapped the touch screen hoping to bring it to life and beginning a much needed charging session. Regardless of what he did, the touch screen on the first station remained blank. Noticing the screen on the second was showing some signs of life, he then clicked away at the options available to him. He pushed through the touchscreen confirming the charge session.

"Maybe this one will work," He said, pulling the hose to the charging port.

He unplugged the broken cable before inserting the second option. Again, nothing happened. No beeps, no bells, no whistles or chimes signaling that a charge had begun.

"Son of a bitch," He screamed. "Can't anything work? Seriously. Stay here. I'm going to head inside and see if there's anything we can do to get these working. Do you want anything from inside? A drink, what?"

"Maybe a bottle of iced tea? If they have anything decent, that is."

"Want any food?" He asked, looking over his shoulder as he walked.

"No, thanks."

Mr. Miller pulled the steel framed glass door open and entered the mini mart. As the door shut behind him, a bell jingled against the glass signaling a customer had arrived. The same smells that greeted Brad,

Jenna and their friends met him. A strangling mix of chemical cleaner on the sticky floors, that damp air from the air conditioning and ice machine and an overall restroom stank that wafted throughout.

Standing behind the counter again was the young towny who had met the teens days earlier. Again, the kid wore his oversized red polo shirt with the gas station logo embroidered on the left chest. His tattoos on full display for everyone to see, and his greasy hair hanging low over his face. He was leaning against the side of the counter flicking through a cell phone when Thomas entered. He didn't bother to look up or greet him, and Thomas didn't care. Thomas went to the wall of glass doors that displayed various racks of sodas, water bottles and other drinks in search of a suitable iced tea for his wife. From one rack he pulled down a large bottle of water for himself. From another, he retrieved a generous sized glass bottle of Tejava for Tammy. As he approached the counter, the clerk didn't bother to look up at him. Thomas stood momentarily, staring at the worker.

"Ahem," He coughed out, slamming both bottles onto the counter. "Excuse me. I don't mean to bother you, but, uh, could I get a little help?"

"Sure man," The clerk said with zero enthusiasm, putting his phone into his pocket. "What's up, man?"

"What's up? Is that how you talk to all your customers?"

"Basically."

"Basically, huh? Well, you've sure got a bright future ahead of you."

"Whatever man. Is this going to be it?" He asked as he scanned the two drinks.

"No, that won't be it. Actually, I need you to turn on the charging station out back. Don't care which. I just need one of them turned on so I can get the hell out of this town."

"Sorry man, those things don't work. That'll be $5.25."

"Whoa, whoa. Hold on a second. What do you mean they don't work?"

"Like I said, man. They're both broken. Have been for a while dude. Sorry. It's $5.25 for the drinks."

"So, what am I supposed to do with my car? It's dead! Is there another charging station in town?"

"Not that I know of. But you know what? Some dude was in here a few days ago or something. Yeah. He was asking about a charging station, too. I think they found one up the freeway a bit. Off Halloran Summit Road."

"Well, if my car is dead, how am I supposed to get it to Halloran Summit Road?"

"I don't know. Maybe call a tow truck?" He said, staring at Thomas intently. "Now, it's $5.25 for the drinks, dude."

"Fucking tow truck," Thomas muttered as he removed his wallet from his back pocket. "Say, what's this all about?"

Thomas pointed at a small, wire display stand that sat on the counter. On the rack hung different packages of beef jerky in four different flavors.

"Oh that. Yeah, that's Herkey Jerky."

"Herkey Jerky?" Thomas asked with a laugh. "What is that, some sort of terrible desert person joke?"

"Nah, some local dude makes it. It's amazing. Best jerky I've ever eaten. I recommend it to everyone that comes in. It'll blow your mind, man."

"Really? Locally made jerky, huh? He has a permit to sell it here?"

"I don't know. He just comes in and drops it off. Lucky for you, he was just in here a bit ago. Just dropped these packs off. As fresh as it gets, dude."

"Huh. Well, I'll take a pack or two. Why not? I've got a long drive ahead of me. Not to mention I now have to get my car towed. I could use a little protein boost. I didn't even get to have my morning shake."

Thomas began admiring the packages and checking out the different flavors that were offered of this highly recommended Herkey Jerky.

"Here we go. I'll take a Hot n Spicy and a Teriyaki."

"Good choices, man. That'll be $14.75."

Thomas swiped his credit card, packed up his drinks and fresh jerky and made his way back to the parking lot to tell Tammy the discouraging news. He pressed the water bottle into the back pocket of his pants, tucked the bottle of tea under his left arm and tore open the bag of Hot n Spicy jerky. He pulled out the first, moist morsel and took a large bite of the meat. Pulling with his hands, his teeth ripped and tore at the tasty, spicy meat strip. His mouth burst with all the flavors packed and jammed into the threads of that jerky. Fresh red pepper intermingling with a dash of honey sweetness and lime paraded around his taste buds like a symphony.

"Holy shit," He said out loud as he approached Tammy.

"What is it?"

"This jerky. Holy shit, babe. It's the best I've ever eaten. Here, try some," He said, handing the bottle of tea over, and offering the bag of meat.

"No, thank you. I don't want to eat a giant strip of beef."

"Suit yourself. More for me. Wow, this is fucking incredible. Super fresh too. The clerk said the guy who makes it just dropped these bags off today."

"What is that? It smells strong."

"Hot n Spicy. This is the freshest jerky I've ever eaten. I should've bought more."

"They sell jerky in San Francisco. You can get more when we get home."

"Not like this, they don't," He said, tearing another morsel from the strip. "By the way. The charging stations are dead. I need to call a tow truck. I guess I can get to a station a few exits up. Say, why don't you fill up the Range Rover here and head on back home. You don't need to wait in the desert with me."

"You sure? I can sit with you. I guess that would be fine."

"You guess?" He asked with a laugh. "No, really. I've punished you with my presence long enough. Head home, I've got my phone and jerky to keep me busy."

They kissed each other before Tammy entered the SUV and made her way back to the freeway. What she didn't tell her husband was that she wouldn't be going home. Not a chance. She was determined to find her children, no matter how long it might take in the bustling city. Deep down, she thought Thomas could be correct with his assumption. They're teenagers. Teenagers can be fickle and unreliable. But a small part of her felt something wasn't right. And she needed to know which side of her heart was correct. She passed the on-ramp which led the way to San Francisco, instead, turning left and merging onto the freeway headed straight to Las Vegas.

Thomas stood, watched and waved as she pulled away and out of sight. He pulled his phone from his pocket and searched for a tow company to call.

"Yes, hello. I need a tow," He said, tearing another piece of tasty meat from the Hot n Spicy strip. "I'm at the truck stop right off the exit for Baker. It's the, uh, Roadrunner Truck Stop. I need to tow my car up to Halloran Summit Road."

CHAPTER 33

A massive, white tow truck chugged along the freeway and clicked on its right blinker to exit at Halloran Summit Road. It coughed and sputtered its way up the incline of the off ramp before turning right and heading out into the vast openness of the desert. Thomas didn't speak much on the drive. He didn't feel the need to speak. An ever-present feeling of shame and embarrassment washed over his entire body from being found in this situation. It did nothing more than make his blood boil even hotter at his son, Brad. In his eyes, this was his fault. He had done this to his family. The anger of being stuck in the middle of nowhere was amplified only by the thought of being let down by his son. In his eyes, this was a constant. He wasn't the problem - His kids were the problem.

The driver had no intention of speaking to Thomas, either. From his clothes, to his attitude, to him rudely chewing away and those bags of meat with his mouth open. The tow driver knew this wasn't someone in which he had much, if anything, in common. He wore a full body jumpsuit that mechanics wear. It was light gray with black pinstripes, and on the left chest was a patch that said Hal. He was fine resigning himself to a quiet drive up the road. Besides, he was going to overcharge Mr. Miller anyway. As he shifted gears to slow down, the tow truck stuttered and jumped multiple times as it approached the lonesome parking lot. Thomas shot a look filled with annoyance in his direction, but he didn't care or show any sign of noticing. As he pulled onto the fresh asphalt, he knew their relationship, as non-existent as it was, had ended.

"Welp, here we are," Hal said. "I'll drop your car and you can do whatever it is you need to do."

"Thanks," Thomas muttered without much emotion.

They both stepped out of the truck, jumping down to the smooth, fresh asphalt below. Hal undid the chains holding the Zeus on the flatbed before allowing it to roll safely back and off the truck. Wasting no time, Hal raised the flat bed and replaced all the chains so he could move on with his evening. The sun was quickly setting, and he wanted to get home to his own wife and kids. Whatever this city boy was up to, well, it was none of his concern.

"Alright my friend," Hal said, wiping his hands on the chest of his jumpsuit. "That'll be $150 and I take cards. How would you like to pay?"

"$150 for a 10-minute tow? Are you shitting me?"

"Hey, it's technically an afterhours job. I was on my way home for the day. $150 it is. Unless you want me to put it up on the truck and take it back?"

"Wouldn't that take more of your time?"

"I don't mind," Hal said, as he spit at the ground. The spit landed right in front of where Thomas stood. And from where Thomas stood, he didn't want to try Hal. He was a big country boy. $150 was more than worth whatever else this man could deliver.

"Alright, fine. $150 it is. Can you at least help me push it closer to the charging stations? The hoses won't reach."

"Hmm," Hal groaned, looking over his right shoulder. He spit at the ground again. "Throw in another $50 and I'll do it."

"$50 to help me push a car? It's electric! A big guy like you? You won't even break a sweat."

Hal stood his ground and didn't say another word. Thomas immediately backed down.

"Fine. I'll throw in another $50. $200 total. And were square? Right?"

"Sure, we're square."

Thomas swiped his card through a credit card reader attached to Hal's phone and then jumped into the front seat of the Zeus. Hal positioned himself at the rear of the car. As soon as Thomas threw it into neutral, Hal started pushing. Thomas wasn't kidding. The electric car was light, and Hal moved it with almost no effort. Easiest $50 he ever swindled out of a city boy like him.

Hal wished him a good evening before riding off into the sunset in his massive, sputtering tow truck. Thomas swiped his credit card inside the charging machine, plugged the dock into the port of the Zeus and watched as the car started coming back to life with juice.

"This should only take about an hour," He said, checking the time on his phone. "I can waste an hour."

He surveyed the area around him for a moment. Aside from an abandoned garage and three seemingly abandoned trailers in the distance, there was nothing as far as the eye could see in this wasteland. He thought it could be interesting - or would at least pass the time - to look around the abandoned garage and store. Thomas walked across the parking lot and stepped onto the sand, climbed over the low cinder block wall and began taking in the old building.

"What a weird location for a garage," He said to himself out loud. "I guess they could help with an oil leak or a burst tire. Who knows?"

He pulled down the sleeve of his jacket and wiped one of the dusty windows as he tried to see inside. The years and years of dirt, dust and elements made the glass so scratched and cloudy, it was impossible.

"Oh well," He said out loud again. "Nothing for me in there, anyway."

He continued to his right and walked around the side of the crumbling building. He considered the kind of people who must have opened this place way out here in the middle of nowhere. An untapped market of potential, maybe? Cheap enough for a Podunk redneck to afford? Seemed more likely in his closed off mind.

He reached the far edge of the building and stepped out into the open. He continued to look the building up and down, checking how damaged and decayed it was. It shocked him that it had lasted this long in the scorching summer sun, the frigid desert winters and all the dust storms and animals that must have claimed it as their own.

Just then, he heard a sound in the distance. A low *THWIP* sound shot out across the landscape. As the sound hit his ears, he was struck by immense pain. A pain so severe, it was like one he had never felt before in his life. Something had struck him in the throat, puncturing the right side of his neck and had burst through the other side. The dead silence was now replaced with throaty gurgles as he reached for gaping wounds. He wrapped both hands around his neck, as he felt warm liquid pour over both his hands and soaking the arms of his jacket. He fought like hell to catch his breath, but it was dissipating faster than his brain could recognize what had occurred.

He fell to the ground landing flat on his back. Blood drained from the open wound on the right side of his neck, as the warm, crimson liquid spilled out from the sides of his mouth. He gasped for air as blood flooded deep into his lungs. He opened and closed his mouth frantically like a fish that had been left on a dock, as his eyes blinked over and over.

Soon, he heard footsteps approaching from his right. He tried to turn his head, but the object that had struck him was so long, it dug into the sand and prevented any movement. Above him stood the figure of a man. He was round, his face distorted and the left side of his body seemed to not quite agree with the other half. It was Herkey. Herkey stood over him, watching the life flood from his eyes as though he had paid admission to do so.

"Help," Thomas gurgled, reaching his right hand up towards Herkey. "Pl-please. Help. Help me."

"I can't believe it," Herkey grumbled, the throaty, gravel filled voice booming off the wall the abandoned garage. He pulled the string back and positioned a new arrow in his crossbow. "I fixed my crossbow. Oh boy, how I've missed playing with my toys."

He pointed the crossbow downward and released the arrow. It shot with extreme force, hitting Thomas directly between the eyes and forcing its way through to the other side of his skull.

Herkey flung the crossbow over his back before bending down and fixing his hands underneath Thomas' limp arms. He wrestled his lifeless body up and into his wheelbarrow before pushing him across the sand towards his trailers. When he reached the first trailer, he opened the door. It flung open, slamming itself into the metal, rusted siding. He pulled Thomas' body up and into the trailer. With each pull, Herkey gave out a labored grunt, as though air was reaching his mouth from his thighs. Deep, painful breaths, each one.

"There we go," Herkey said through gross panting. "More fresh meat for my hungry friends."

CHAPTER 34

Just over a year later...

A black Toyota Highlander had just reached the top of the grade and began the long descent into Primm Valley situated on the state line between California and Nevada. Inside the SUV was the Clark family. Driving was Dad, Jimmy Clark with his salt and pepper hair, clean-shaven face and beer belly that stuck out so far, it almost touched the steering wheel. Next to him sat his wife, Martha. Her black hair pulled into a ponytail with a red visor resting on her forehead. She flipped through a travel guide map they had picked up from a gas station when they were forced to fill up the tank and empty their bladders.

In the back seat were their three children - Michael age 14, Sarah age 12 and Theresa age 9. Michael had AirPods in as he listened to that day's menu of angsty, teenage punk music. Sarah and Theresa, both spitting images of their mother, each flicked their fingers across their respective tablets playing games, searching the internet and chatting with friends.

As they broke over the peak into Primm, through the windshield they could see the small, yet bustling town on the State line. Different hotels and casinos lined the highway inviting travelers in for a quick stay in their luxurious hotel rooms, a trip to the card room and promising the loosest slots and lowest priced buffets this side of Las Vegas. But the Clark family was interested in something else.

"Hey kids, here it is again!" Jimmy belted with excitement, reaching for the radio dial and pumping the volume to an uncomfortably loud level.

The girls in the back let out a collective "Yay!" at what played over the speakers. A radio commercial with a vintage, yet creepy vibe echoed throughout the car. First, it opened with electronic music straight out of the 1980s with female voices singing in unison—

The wind and the sun in your face.
So much fun and flavor in just one place.
Where else in the desert can you have so much fun?
Herkey Farms!

The music continued, though the singing voices were replaced by the throaty voice of an older man—

Stop on by and visit Herkey Farms.
There's a whole new dimension of fun now open in the Desert.
Herkey Farms.

The singing women then chimed back in—

Come for the rides, stay for a meal.
At such low prices, it's almost a steal.

Followed again by the old man's gravelly voice—

Cool off on Mr. Herkey's Bumper Boats.
Ride a majestic unicorn on the Merry Go Round.
Even see heights never seen before from the top of Herkey's Ferris wheel.
And Now open - Don't miss the Tenderizer, a brand-new roller-coaster attraction for all ages.
Herkey Farms. Located at Exit one in Primm, Nevada. Three miles East up Primm Valley Road.

Before the commercial ended, the female singers finished off the dreadful song—

So much Family fun
Happening in the desert sun
Visit Herkey Farms today!

When the commercial finished, everyone in the SUV cheered with immense joy. All but 14-year-old Michael, who, if he cared any less about this farm, he might die right where he sat.

"Are you guys excited?" Asked Martha. "We're almost at Herkey Farms!"

"Thank god," Jimmy said. "Lord knows, after this drive, I need a meal."

"Well don't you worry honey. Mr. Herkey will take great care of you."

"I want to ride the Tenderizer!" Shouted 9-year-old Theresa.

"We'll see," Martha said with caution. "Let's make sure that you're tall enough. And if so, we're *all* going to ride it!"

More collective cheers from everyone except Michael.

"Hey, Mikey," Jimmy shouted.

"What, Dad?" Michael asked, removing the AirPods from his ears.

"Aren't you excited?"

"No, why should I be? I'm on a family trip going to some farm in the middle of nowhere that is known for beef jerky. Who cares?"

"Hey, come on now," Martha shouted. "Don't ruin the fun for everyone else. Right girls?"

"Yeah, stupid," Theresa yelled at Michael.

When they reached exit 1 in Primm, they pulled off the freeway and proceeded to Primm Valley Road. They took a right and drove past the enormous hotels and casinos, choosing instead to visit the newly opened Herkey Farms.

When they arrived, they turned left into a dirt parking lot on the outskirts of the farm. It was a sprawling park that stretched deep into the desert. At the entrance was a larger-than-life clay statue of Mr. Herkey holding a pitchfork standing next to a giant cow. His left hand was placed on the cow's head, as though he was petting it. As if, somehow, they were friends. The family walked under an archway that was lined with carnival lights of all different colors that flashed and blinked in an inviting manner.

To the right was the main restaurant of the farm. It was a rustic building made of old wood to resemble a log cabin. Inside, wooden tables stretched deep into the building, as families sat around eating dinner. The menu featured many country style dishes, all which, as advertised, were made fresh daily from ingredients from the farm. Including of course, all the meat that was served. No outside meats were ever to be trucked into the farm. All the meat butchered and served had to be raised on premises. It was a Herkey policy. A Herkey guarantee to his guests. From pork chops to meatloaf all the way to smoked burgers and fresh, handmade sausages. And if you felt like splurging, they even served what they considered the freshest filet mignon in the valley.

To the left of the restaurant sat all the rides. From the merry-go-round, to the Ferris wheel, even a tilt a whirl. Far off to the left, almost at the edge of the farm was a large pool of water with bumper boats zipping back and forth as families crashed into one another in an attempt at both fun and beating some of the summer heat. At the far end of the farm was the highly anticipated Tenderizer roller coaster. It stretched high up into the sky and boasted a deep drop that made the meat you had just eaten rise from your stomach to your throat in an instant. In the middle of it all was a general store that served soda pop, old world style candies, fudge and of course, fresh Herkey Jerky.

At the furthest point of the farm, way out back, guests could see the famous Herkey farmhouses. Three wooden structures stood next to one another, the largest set in the middle. Surrounding the farmhouses were tall chain-link fences. Smack in the middle was a door made of chain-link that swung outward. The door was padlocked and chained shut with a billboard sized sign stating "NO ADMITTANCE".

"Wow, this place is better than I imagined," Jimmy shouted, his eyes wide open and his stomach rumbling with hunger.

"I love it, Dad!" Theresa yelled.

"Me too, thank you for bringing us!" Sarah said, bouncing up and down with excitement.

"Michael, can you at least pretend to have some fun with the family? Come on now. At least enjoy the meal with us."

"Fine," Michael said with a long roll of the eyes. "Hey guys, look at that. Isn't that Mr. Herkey himself?"

"It is," Jimmy said as he waved. "Hey Mr. Herkey!"

Mr. Herkey came racing down one of the many dirt paths in a bright green golf cart, waving and greeting visitors as he drove.

"Welcome everyone! Hello everyone! Enjoy your stay. And don't fill up on the bread. Leave some room for the freshest meat you've ever tasted!"

Herkey drove the cart through the farm grounds, waving and smiling at the visitors as he went. He made his way through all the fun and excitement and drove towards the farmhouses positioned at the back of the farm. When he reached the chain-link door, he jumped out of the cart and scooted his awkward body to the padlock. Quickly he unlocked it, walked inside and replaced the padlock, locking himself inside the chain-link fence.

He waddled his body up the path to the largest of the three barns. Each was made of dark woods and stretched high into the sky. On the front of each were double barn doors, tall enough for a large tractor to enter. He grabbed the handle of the right door and dragged it open. The wood and hinges creaked as it opened, and he waddled his body inside, shutting the door behind him. On the side of the interior wall sat an electric box that was mounted on the wood. He reached and flicked the light switch, as electricity crackled and hummed, illuminating the interior.

From the front all the way to the back, and stretching from left to right, were small stalls that had been built to house the animals before slaughter. But this wasn't your typical farm with cows, sheep, pigs and horses. No, this was Herkey's farm. Chained inside each of those stalls were hundreds of human beings. Adults, children and everything in between. Herkey's own personal collection. His fresh meat which was to be served daily to the farm's unsuspecting guests. Each person was hogtied with their heads pressed out through the wooden slats. A ball gag was strapped into each of their mouths. When the light flicked on, each stall boomed to life as his prisoners fought like hell to loosen the ties that bound them.

To his right was his trusty meat hook hanging on a nail stuck into the wood. He picked up the meat hook and began walking down the center row of stalls. He didn't stop to look at any of the people he had captured and held captive, almost as though he didn't even notice them. Like it didn't faze him in the slightest. And clearly, it didn't. When he got to the end of the row, he stopped and looked to his right.

In this particular stall was a large, porky pig looking man. If one had to guess, he appeared over 6 feet tall and close to 280 pounds. Herkey glared down at him, his crooked eyes shook and his black smile widened.

"You know what time it is," Herkey grumbled.

The man shook violently, hoping for any last-ditch effort to escape. To get away from the fate before him. But it was no use.

"The restaurant is out of pork chops, piggy," Herkey said.

He slid the meat hook underneath the man's throat, slashing upwards as the hook sliced his flesh from just below his jaw all the way to his left ear. Blood burst from his neck, pouring onto the dirt creating a large black mass as it pooled and mixed with the accumulated filth. As every drop of blood from the man's body continued to flood from his neck, Herkey waddled to the back wall of the barn. Pressed against the dark wood slats was a band saw for cutting meat, tendon and bone. Herkey leaned over the best his body would allow and flicked the saw's power on. It shrieked and whined as the blade spun, waiting patiently for something to pulverize.

"Can't leave the guests hungry, no," Herkey said, staring back at the now lifeless man. "No, we can't leave the guests hungry. We must feed the guests."

THE END

ACKNOWLEDGEMENTS

Thank You to Tabitha for always supporting whatever wild idea I may come up with and always being my number one fan. Thanks for always pushing me to keep working no matter how beat down I may feel. Thank You to Wilma, Rufus and Sidney for being the sweetest support babies that have ever graced this planet. Thank You to my Mom, Lohn, Dad and Janien for always being there for me, no matter how hard I have made it at times. Same goes for Audra, Chet, Rebekah, Delilah and Ephraim. Thank You for being you, and for loving me for me, always.

A huge Thank You and High Fives to - JulieAnne, Matthew and Stormy, the Zirpolo Family, the Van Sickles, The Servis and Gelsomino families, Raylee for the laughs and believing in me. The entire Oasis Beer Club and Crew. Duddy, Steve, Bill, (evil) Matt, Mike, Noah and Thomas for being true brothers through it all. A special Thank You to anyone who bought, read and shared/reviewed Bone Saw Serenade, and to all friends and family that believed in, supported or at least tolerated me over the years. Thank You from the bottom of my heart. Also, The Golden State Warriors and San Diego Padres. Get those rings.

Thank You to Reagan and the Black Rose Family for making this dream a reality. I will forever be indebted to your trust, confidence and dedication to the craft. And to anyone who bought, found, borrowed and read this book. Thank You, Thank You, THANK YOU. You have contributed, knowingly or not, in making a dream come true. And for that, I will be forever thankful.

To anyone and everyone out there with a dream - Get out and make it happen. Don't ever let anyone tell you what you can or can't do. Let nothing stand in your way. The book you are currently holding in your hands is proof that dreams can come true. Now, go make yours happen. And to anyone who feels or has ever felt unseen or unheard - May the brightest, most beautiful light shine upon you and allow the world to see how truly amazing you are. You got this.

If you read this story - Thank You. Much Love, Always.

ABOUT THE AUTHOR

Cody J. Thompson is from San Diego, California. He is the author of thriller *Bone Saw Serenade*, published by Black Rose Writing. Previously, he wrote as a columnist with his work featured in *San Diego CityBeat*, *San Diego Weekly Reader*, *The Westcoaster Magazine*, *San Diego Downtown News* and he was the staff columnist for *San Diego Uptown News* writing about the beverage industry. With storytelling, he focuses mainly on thriller-inspired work. When he is not writing or reading, he spends time with his wife and their two pit bulls, cheers on his Golden State Warriors and San Diego Padres and can be found writing, producing and hosting the first and longest-running beer podcast in San Diego, *Beer Night in San Diego*.

NOTE FROM THE AUTHOR

Word-of-mouth is crucial for any author to succeed. If you enjoyed *This One's Gonna Hurt*, please leave a review online—anywhere you are able. Even if it's just a sentence or two. It would make all the difference and would be very much appreciated.

Thanks!
Cody J. Thompson

We hope you enjoyed reading this title from:

www.blackrosewriting.com

Subscribe to our mailing list – *The Rosevine* – and receive **FREE** books, daily deals, and stay current with news about upcoming releases and our hottest authors.
Scan the QR code below to sign up.

Already a subscriber? Please accept a sincere thank you for being a fan of Black Rose Writing authors.

View other Black Rose Writing titles at
www.blackrosewriting.com/books and use promo code
PRINT to receive a **20% discount** when purchasing.

CPSIA information can be obtained
at www.ICGtesting.com
Printed in the USA
BVHW082028160223
658686BV00013B/301